"We
such

Will went on, "You've got the wrong
impression of us. Our differences have been on
a purely business level. Your mistake was
taking it personally. I've told you that before,
but you still don't believe me. Your ranch
happens to sit on land I want. If you had
bought any other place, I would have wished
you the best of luck."

His fingers slowly stroked the underside of her
jaw, tracing its firm set. Edie shut her eyes at
the raw ache his caress induced. Her fingers
closed over his forearm to draw his hand away.

"Which doesn't change the fact that we still own
the ranch, Maddock," she said firmly, "and we
aren't going to sell."

Edie knew her land was safe from Will
Maddock—but her heart certainly was not....

JANET DAILEY AMERICANA

Janet Dailey
Americana

DAKOTA
DREAMIN'

Harlequin Books

TORONTO • NEW YORK • LONDON
AMSTERDAM • PARIS • SYDNEY • HAMBURG
STOCKHOLM • ATHENS • TOKYO • MILAN

The state flower depicted on the cover of this book is pasqueflower.

Janet Dailey Americana edition published February 1988
Second printing October 1988
Third printing October 1989
Fourth printing October 1990
Fifth printing December 1991
Sixth printing September 1992
Seventh printing October 1992

ISBN 0-373-89891-6

Harlequin Presents edition published August 1981

Original hardcover edition published in 1981
by Mills & Boon Limited

DAKOTA DREAMIN'

CHAPTER ONE

FINGERS OF SHOCK continued to send tingles down her spine as Edie Gibbs stared at the check in her hands. Her mind refused to assimilate the number of digits in the dollar figure. She lifted a hand to touch her fingertips to her temple and let them glide into her soft brown hair.

"I...I don't think I quite understand, Mr. Wentworth." At last she found her voice, husky though it was, to address the lawyer sitting in the wing-backed chair her late husband had always occupied. "When you phoned and asked to discuss my...my financial condition, I thought—" A bewildered laugh escaped her throat. "It took all of our savings to pay the funeral costs. Here I've been worrying how I was going to earn enough money to keep the house. I thought you were going to inform me about a monumental pile of debts. But this?" Her confused hazel eyes sought the attorney's face as she lifted the check in a questioning fashion. "Is it real?"

"I assure you it is very real." The gentleness in his expression said he was pleased his news was good.

"But I didn't know Joe had any insurance." Edie stared at the slip of paper that represented so much money. "We talked about it a long time ago, but we couldn't squeeze the premium payments into our budget." Which raised another question. Again her gaze lifted to the attorney in curious demand. "Where did Joe get the money to pay them?"

"I was just coming to that." He opened the briefcase sitting on his lap and took out a sheaf of papers.

"May I look at that, mom?" Her daughter reached over to take the check from her numbed fingers. The action drew an abstracted glance from Edie that touched the pony-tailed girl seated on the couch before her attention was claimed by the documents the attorney was handing her. She glanced through them, but the legal jargon was beyond her comprehension.

"What does all this mean?" Again her hazel eyes darkened with confusion.

"I believe your late husband did a lot of tinkering in his workshop," he began.

"That's an understatement," Edie declared in a silent and rueful laugh. "Joe spent nearly every spare minute he had in his workshop. He'd come home from the garage, shower, eat and disappear into the shed until it was bedtime." There was nothing malicious or resentful in her statement. It had been too much a part of the accepted routine. "He loved working there. That was his escape."

"It was a profitable escape. In with those documents there are registrations of patents, some of which your late husband was able to sell to auto manufacturers in Detroit," John Wentworth explained.

"Patents?" Edie was beginning to think she would never escape this whirl of confusion. None of this was making any sense. "Joe didn't even have a high-school diploma." Something he had been very self-conscious about. Without it he hadn't been able to obtain any job other than that of a garage mechanic, a trade at which he had excelled, but hadn't found much pride in. "He tried. He took night courses at school whenever he could, but...." Edie let the sentence trail off unfinished to gaze at the documents she held.

"Whatever your late husband lacked in formal education, he more than made up for in natural inventiveness," the attorney assured her. "The royalties off these patents will provide you with a very comfortable income for a good many years, Mrs. Gibbs. Plus I have a national firm negotiating to purchase the rights on two more of his patents."

This was more than she could take in. The silence from her daughter and stepson indicated they, too, were finding these announcements difficult to comprehend.

"I don't understand." She shook her head in bewilderment, the softly curling length of her brown hair barely brushing her shoulders.

"Why . . . why didn't Joe tell me . . . tell us about these patents?"

"I really can't answer that," John Wentworth sighed. "I know he seemed very self-conscious about his inventions, as if they were a fluke. He was determined that no one should know about them."

"And the money from these patents went to pay the premiums on the insurance policy?" Edie made the statement into a question, seeking a reconfirmation of his earlier explanation.

"The vast majority of it, yes," the attorney nodded. "He seemed determined that you would be taken care of in the event anything happened to him. It was almost as if he had a premonition." He removed another set of papers from his briefcase and handed them to Edie. "These are a summary and a projection of your annual income under the present agreements."

He leaned forward to go over them with her. Edie listened and followed his moving finger down the list, but it was all a haze, something not quite real. She had been so braced for bad news that being presented with a pot of gold was something that seemed too good to be true.

Beneath her suntanned complexion was a white pallor of shock. Features that were usually so animated with her irrepressible zest to meet life and its problems head-on were blank of expression. Her youthfully slim but mature figure was clad in the somber colors of mourning, but she seemed too young to be a widow, the attorney thought—or to have a grown daughter for that matter. Either way, this very attractive woman was not at all the way he had pictured Joseph Gibbs's wife. But it had been said that opposites attract. He noticed the stunned light in her large eyes.

"Let me make a suggestion, Mrs. Gibbs," he said. "I'll leave these papers for you to look over. You can call me in a couple of days. I'm certain you are going to have some questions, and it would be wise if we discussed the possibility of some financial investments for your future."

"Yes. I would like a few days to think about it," Edie agreed a little numbly and belatedly started to rise.

"I'll walk Mr. Wentworth to the door, Edie," the young man seated on the couch volunteered.

"Thanks, Jerry, and I will call you, Mr. Wentworth," she added.

Her confusion began to sort itself as the front door was opened and closed, but Edie still felt stunned by the unexpected turn of events. At the sound of approaching footsteps, she lifted her gaze from the papers in her hand.

"Did you know about this, Jerry?" It was possible since her stepson had often helped Joe in his workshop on weekends. Her gaze curiously searched his face, his features steady and reliable like his father's. Except his blue eyes often held the twinkle of humor, his mouth smiled easily, and his sandy brown hair was shaggy in a carelessly attractive way.

"I remember once he was trying to modify one of the new emission-control devices, but, no—" he shook his head and paused by her chair to take the papers from her hand and leaf through them "—I didn't know anything about patents."

"You'd better take this check, mom." Alison shoved it into her hands. "I can't believe we have so much money. Last night I couldn't sleep, worrying that I might have to sell one of my horses. Now...we could buy a whole stable full and not put a dent in that check."

"I was afraid we were going to have to sell off the acreage," Edie admitted. "I know we've been able to board enough other horses to pay for the upkeep of our own, but the mortgage payment on this place, the utilities, groceries, all amounted to so much that—"

"You don't have to worry about that now, Edie." Her stepson said the very thought that was echoing through her mind.

"I know," she murmured. "But why didn't he tell us? Why didn't your father tell us?"

"Dad...was too easygoing," Jerry said without criticizing. "You always were the battler in this family, Edie. You managed the money and kept the bill collectors at bay during the hard times. Remember that time I got picked up for drinking on my sixteenth birthday? You were the one who went to bat for me with the judge."

"But what has that got to do with this?" she argued. "Think of how much money it cost him for this insurance policy. We could have used that money...or some of it. We could have taken a vacation or bought a new car," she added, remembering the clunker Joe had always coaxed into running.

"Just before I left for the marines, dad and I had a little talk—really one of the few we ever had. He told me that the one thing he had always regretted was marrying my mother when he was just sixteen. He not only had to quit school and get a job to support her, and later me, but he told me that he had to abandon his dreams." Jerry sat down in the chair the attorney had vacated and leaned forward, clasping his hands together in a thoughtful attitude.

"That was one reason he was always so determined that the two of you had a chance at life." Edie knew that story, and she was warmed by the memory of how profoundly her late husband had meant it. "He told me that, too."

"What he probably didn't tell you," her stepson continued, "was that he felt guilty for marrying you."

"Guilty?" She was startled. "Why?"

"After my mother died in that car accident, dad didn't know how to cope with raising a kid on his own. Then he met you, Edie. He married you a week after you graduated from high school. He said he stole your dreams, too. Right away you had a child to raise, debts to pay, a living to earn and no time to be young and in love."

"But Joe needed me. So did you," Edie protested. "I never felt that I missed anything."

"It always bothered him that the two of you never had a honeymoon," Jerry added.

"We had a honeymoon, a belated one," she insisted. "Don't you remember that camping trip we all took to the Black Hills?"

"What kind of honeymoon is that?" Alison laughed affectionately. "You had two nosy kids along. It could hardly be classified as romantic by any stretch of the imagination."

"Joe wasn't a very romantic person," Edie admitted. It was the truth, and she didn't feel she was being unkind to his memory to say so. His other qualities had more than made up for his lack of sentimentality. Anyone who had ever known Joseph Gibbs had loved him, herself included. Honesty about his faults wouldn't diminish what he'd been.

"To answer the question that started all this discussion," Jerry inserted, "I think dad did what he did, and the way he did it, because he wanted you to be able to have your dreams, Edie, if anything ever happened to him."

The telephone rang and Alison bolted from the couch. "I'll get it!" As she raced to answer it, she ignored the extension in the living room in favor of the privacy offered by the kitchen phone. "It might be Craig." The quick explanation was tossed over her shoulder.

Edie watched the slim, long-legged girl sprint from the room. "She hasn't heard from Craig since the funeral," she murmured to Jerry, referring to the boy Alison had been dating steadily since spring graduation, Craig Gurney.

"She won't, either." His face wore a very adult expression, revealing all of his twenty-four years of experience and more.

"Why?" Obviously her stepson knew something neither she nor Alison did.

"The word's out. Since Alison wouldn't deliver, Gurney is looking for a girl who will," he said grimly. "She's well rid of him, but I doubt if she will agree. Don't tell her what I said. I don't think Alison realizes how much guys talk."

"I won't."

"And let me know if Craig tries to see her again. I want to have a little talk with him if he does."

It didn't take much reading between the lines to guess what Jerry would talk to him about. He'd always been very protective toward Alison since the day Edie had brought her home from the hospital. The two shared a rare relationship for siblings. Rivalry between them was nonexistent. Alison idolized her older half-brother and Jerry had long ago put his baby sister on a pedestal. Their closeness had always been a great source of pride and pleasure for Edie.

"Mom?" Alison stuck her head around the kitchen door. "It's Mrs. Van Doren." She wrinkled her nose in dislike. "She wants to know how soon you are going to have her sofa and chair reupholstered. I explained about dad's funeral and all. To hear her talk, you'd think dad picked a terribly inconvenient time to die—the old prune face."

Edie smothered a sigh of irritation and tried to remember how much work was left on the items. "Tell her I'll have them finished by Friday."

"I'll tell her." Alison disappeared behind the door.

Upholstering furniture in her home had been one of the ways Edie had supplemented their income. Joe's salary had barely been able to stretch to meet their necessities. With the house, the garden and taking care of the horses they boarded on the acreage, it hadn't been feasible for Edie to have a job in town. But she had discovered there were any number of things she could do at home to earn extra money.

"There's something I didn't make clear when we were talking a minute ago about the money dad left you," Jerry said. "He left it for you, Edie. Not for me or Alison. You are the only mother I've ever known. I may not call you that, but you are. I don't want you to think that we need any of that money...or should have any of it."

"But—" She attempted a protest.

But Jerry interrupted, "I mean it. You are only thirty-six, Edie. You are a very attractive woman with your whole life ahead of you yet.''

"You are very good for my ego, Jerry," Edie smiled, and would have continued, but he wouldn't let her.

"Dad wanted you to have it. I know I speak for Alison when I say that we want you to have it. We know how much you've sacrificed for us. How long has it been since you bought a new dress?'' he challenged.

"How long has it been since I needed a new one?'' she joked, because her husband hadn't been the type to party or go out for an evening, even if they could have afforded it. He preferred a home-cooked meal to any restaurant fare.

"With that money—'' he gestured toward the check in her hand ''—you can buy yourself a whole new wardrobe, travel, have fun, do anything you want.'' As he was making the statement, Alison reentered the living room in time to hear it.

"There's something else you can do, too, mom," she inserted, pausing to sit on the arm of Edie's chair. "I was thinking about it in the kitchen after I hung up from talking to Mrs. Van Doren. You could open up your own upholstery shop, go into business for yourself. Everybody around here knows how good you are at it.''

Own her own business? Edie considered the idea, then dismissed it with a slight shake of her head. "It would mean having a shop in town and spending most of the day inside when I'd rather be outdoors. No, I don't think I'd like that, in spite of the challenge. As for traveling, there are a lot of places I'd like to see, but—'' She sighed without finishing the statement, because she doubted if she would find much enjoyment in sightseeing alone. There would always be the memory of how much fun they'd had as a family on that camping trip to the Black Hills of South Dakota and the instantaneous love she had felt for that Indian land.

"It isn't anything you have to decide now," Jerry reminded her.

"No. And I don't intend to make any rash decisions about it, either," she smiled firmly.

"I would be surprised if you did, Edie," Jerry declared, and pushed his lanky frame upright. "It's just about chore time so I'd better get back to the farm." Since he had returned home after his tour of enlistment with the marines, Jerry had worked for a large, corporate-owned farm with an enormous acreage of crops as well as a cattle-feedlot operation.

"I'm glad you could get time off from work to come over while the attorney was here," Edie said.

"Yeah, well, it was too wet to be in the fields today anyhow, so—'' He shrugged away the rest of the sentence.

"Speaking of chores," Edie glanced at her daughter, "we have some horses that need to be grained."

"And stalls to be cleaned," Alison grimaced. "I'd better go change clothes."

"Me, too," Edie agreed, glancing down at her brown dress.

Jerry had started toward the front door. "I'll probably be over Sunday, unless we start haying."

"Sunday dinner will be at one o'clock, as always," Edie told him before she followed Alison up the stairs to the bedrooms on the second floor.

After the front screen door had slammed shut, the engine of Jerry's pickup roared to life in the yard of the old farmhouse. Edie paused at the open door of her daughter's bedroom. She watched for a silent second as Alison dragged a pair of worn blue jeans and an old shirt from her closet. It didn't seem possible that Alison would be eighteen in two short months.

"Did you want something, mom?" Alison glanced up to see her standing in the doorway.

"I was just wondering—" she began, and changed to a more direct approach. "Do you want to go to college, Alison?"

"I thought we'd been through all that." She widened her brown eyes in mock exasperation.

"I know we talked about it before you graduated, but—" Edie paused "—I want to be certain you refused because you didn't want to go and not because you knew we couldn't afford it. With the insurance money—"

"No, mom," Alison interrupted firmly. "I

don't want to go to college. I'm not college material. Look at my grades. Besides, I'm like my dad. I don't have any ambition beyond having a nice home and family someday.''

"I don't think you are being exactly fair about your father.'' Edie was immediately defensive, because she knew too well the night courses Joe had taken in an attempt to better himself.

"Yes, I am,'' Alison insisted. "I know why dad never said anything about those inventions of his. He didn't want people to treat him like someone he wasn't. He was just a mechanic—a good one, but just a mechanic. He wasn't ashamed of it, and neither am I.''

"That doesn't explain why he didn't tell us.'' Edie returned to the question that kept nagging her.

"Don't you see, mom? If he had told you, you would have been so proud of him you would have told everybody. Can you imagine how someone like Mrs. Van Doren would have started fawning over him, saying how clever he was. Dad couldn't have stood that. Dad just wasn't the type that ever wanted to be the center of attention.''

"Yes, I suppose you're right,'' Edie sighed, seeing the logic of her daughter's explanation.

In a town the size of this small Illinois community, Joe's inventions would have been big news. And Joe couldn't have coped with being a minor celebrity. Heavens, he hadn't even been able to cope with raising a small boy on his own, yet he had been such a strong, stalwart man in many ways.

"Look at me. I'm good with animals—breaking and training horses and such," Alison continued as she untied her wraparound skirt, tossed it on the bed and tugged on her jeans. "I know you once mentioned I could become a veterinarian, but all that anatomy stuff is beyond me. I can't even pronounce some of the diseases, let alone spell them. But, between the money I got from selling Fiesta's colt and what I'll be able to save working as a carhop at the drive-in this summer, I'll be able to pay for that horseshoeing course this fall. Then we won't have the expense of shoeing our horses, plus I can make extra money by shoeing the horses we board."

"One thing is certain. I don't think we'll ever be without horses," Edie stated with a somewhat wry smile.

"Yeah," Alison agreed, and looked up to reveal the impish twinkle in her brown eyes. "We're both horse crazy. Dad loved them, too," she added, a faint sadness touching her smile before it brightened. "Even if we never could get him to climb on one."

"Yes, that's true."

"You'd better hurry up and get changed, mom." She leaned against the single bed to pull on her boots. "I want to work Fiesta's filly at halter, and I'll probably need your help at first."

"I won't be a minute," Edie promised and moved away from the door to her own room.

It was funny how young Alison seemed to her, yet she had been a few months younger than her when she had married Joe straight out of high school. Edie walked to the closet to remove her old clothes. Now there were only her clothes in the closet; she had given all of Joe's to the church. Not that he'd had many, since he'd rarely worn anything but garage overalls. Their faint greasy odor still lingered in the air. She wondered how long it would take before the smell faded.

While she dressed, her gaze strayed to the framed photographs on the dresser. One, the most recent picture she had, was a picture of the four of them taken ten years ago at Christmas. Everyone was smiling except Joe, whose face was in the shadow of the Christmas tree. The second and third frames held yellowed photographs of her parents and her two brothers, and her grandparents.

Their deaths when Edie was only four were a tragedy still talked about in the small Illinois community; almost an entire family, save Edie, wiped out in a single car accident. At the time of the accident she had been staying with her uncle, who subsequently took her in and raised her with his children. She had always been treated on an equal basis with her cousins, yet Edie had never felt that she truly belonged to their family unit.

In the spring of her senior year at high school she had met Joe. At almost the same time, her uncle had announced that they would be moving to California where he had been transferred with a promotion. Edie hadn't wanted to go. And the more she saw of Joe and five-year-old Jerry, the more she realized how much they needed her . . . and how much she needed them.

All in all, she'd had a good life and a good marriage. She didn't regret it.

THE NEXT THREE MONTHS were an adjustment period for Edie as a single woman again. Although she was used to making most of the decisions since Joe had so often been preoccupied with his work or projects, there had always been the comforting knowledge that she could consult him when a problem arose. Now virtually everything was solely her decision— from what time to get up to what to fix for dinner.

There was one major decision Edie had postponed making—what to do with the money? She had discussed it with John Wentworth, the attorney. And as soon as various friends and acquaintances learned about it, they volunteered suggestions. To this point she had spent only a very tiny portion of it since she had continued to live on the strict budget they'd had before. Nearly all of it was presently secured in an interest-bearing account waiting for her decision.

One thing kept running through her mind whenever she thought about how she should use it. Jerry's comment that Joe had wanted her to have her dreams kept echoing back. At first she had dismissed the possibility because, on the surface, her dream seemed ludicrous and impractical. Although she never discussed it with anyone, not even Jerry or Alison, the idea kept coming back. Each time she found more and more reasons that made it seem plausible.

Finally Edie realized that she had to sound out her idea on Jerry and Alison. She needed their reaction to her proposal. Without their support, she wouldn't be able to achieve her goal. The opportunity came on Sunday when Jerry arrived to have dinner with them.

Having set the platter of roast pork on the table, Edie sat in the chair opposite Jerry, at the head of the table. She waited until Alison had offered the blessing and the food was being passed around.

"Mmm, you outdid yourself today, Edie," Jerry declared, inhaling deeply the fragrant aroma of the sage dressing accompanying the pork. "After a week of eating what comes out of the tin cans Chuck opens, this is manna from heaven."

"Is it true that Craig is going out with Chuck's sister?" Alison demanded.

Jerry measured his half-sister with a sidelong glance then nodded. "Yes, it's true." He helped himself to a heaping mound of mashed potatoes.

"I thought so." It was a somewhat choked response that Alison tried to hide.

"I was cleaning a closet this week and ran across a couple of boxes pushed way to the back. You'll never guess what I found in one of them," Edie stated and didn't make them ask. "Old snapshots of our trip to the Black Hills. They are on the buffet table behind you, Alison."

The distraction was one her daughter sought, and she reached back to remove the packet of photographs from the bureau top. "That old Brownie camera took good pictures, didn't it?" she remarked after she had glanced through the first couple of snapshots. "How old were we, mom? Oh, Jerry, look at this one!" she laughed and instantly handed it to him.

"I think you were eight and Jerry was fourteen," Edie replied.

"You were a bean pole then," Alison teased her brother.

"You were pretty skinny yourself," he retorted good-naturedly.

"Look! This is really a terrific picture of the four faces at Mount Rushmore!" Alison handed him another. "Here's one of the buffalo herd!" As she continued to pass the snapshots on to him, Jerry would sneak a bite of food and lay his silverware down in time to take the next one she handed him. "We had so much fun on that trip," she sighed.

"Do you remember this, Edie?" Jerry handed her one of the pictures, a laughing gleam in his eyes. "You were trying to cook hamburgers on an outdoor grate. They kept breaking in half and falling through onto the coals."

"And Joe kept rescuing them," Edie remembered.

"They were the grittiest hamburgers I've ever eaten," he concluded.

"Definitely not one of my more memorable meals," she agreed with a laugh.

"Would you just look at that country? Isn't it beautiful?" Alison murmured as she handed Jerry a photograph taken of the wild, rolling landscape. "Do you remember how we all started dreaming about owning a ranch there someday? Even dad?"

"Do I remember!" Jerry laughed shortly. "We planned how many acres we were going to have, how many head of cattle it would hold, how much hay ground we would need for winter feed, how many horses we should have. Dad and I were even going to trap in the winter so Edie could have a fur coat."

"You called it our Dakota dream ranch, didn't you, mom?" Alison remembered with a faraway look.

"It doesn't have to be just a dream ranch," Edie said carefully. "We could have it now."

Alison stared at her for a long moment. "We could, couldn't we?" she breathed in realization.

Edie turned her gaze to the young man seated across from her. Astonishment was written in his features. He set his silverware down again, the food on his plate forgotten as he searched her face.

"You are serious about this, aren't you?" His response was almost an accusation.

"Yes." She was holding her breath.

"Do you know how much a ranch out there would cost?" Jerry questioned on a note of disbelief.

"I have a pretty good idea," Edie nodded.

"We can afford it." Alison was giving the idea her full support.

"Even after the down payment there would be enough money left out of the insurance to buy some stock and have a year's working capital." She had already done some rough figuring in her head. "There would still be some money coming in from the patents besides that."

Jerry obviously found it difficult to argue with that. He shook his head and glanced at the photographs scattered across the table amid the bowls of food. "I suppose finding these pictures made you think about it."

"No. I went looking for them, because I remembered what you said about Joe wanting me to use the money to fulfill my dreams," she explained. "Except this isn't just my dream. It was *our* dream. Yours, Alison's, Joe's and mine."

"I think it's the greatest idea I've ever heard," Alison enthused.

"All right." Jerry was still thinking, mulling it all over. It was what Edie wanted him to do. "You can afford it. And it is something you've wanted. But how on earth are you going to run it? What do you know about running a ranch?"

"Most of it is common sense," Edie reasoned. "And I'm not completely without experience, limited though it is. I was raised on my uncle's farm. I've hayed, driven tractors, doctored sick animals, and done a hundred other things. I've certainly had a lot of experience mending fences, and I've been riding horses since I was five. None of that means I can handle the operation of a ranch by myself."

"I'm relieved to hear you admit that." Jerry leaned back in his chair, a vaguely mocking smile curving his mouth.

"However—" Edie paused for effect "—I think I might know where I can get some qualified help to work with me." She glanced at her daughter. "There's you, for instance, Alison. Now that you and Craig are finally through, you might consider coming with me. Between the two of us, we have delivered our share of foals, including the breach birth Fiesta had this last time. Cows can't be that much different. Besides, you have enrolled in that horseshoeing course, a skill that will definitely come in handy on a ranch."

"I'll pack tomorrow, mom," Alison promised.

"What about you, Jerry?" Edie glanced at her stepson, who was the big question mark in her mind. "You are the one with the experience. You've worked practically every summer on the farm with that feedlot operation. You have all the first-hand knowledge about cattle. Is there someone special here you wouldn't want to leave?" Since he had moved out she knew very little about his social life, except that he dated, but she didn't know of any girl he was dating steadily.

"No. There is no one special," he admitted, and Edie could see he was weakening.

"There is one thing I would want clear from the very start," she said. "This is going to be a family ranch, especially if we are all working for it. We'll all have an interest in it and a share of the profits, if there are any.

"Thanks to your father, I don't *have* to do anything. It's what I want and what I think is fair. The two of you are going to work just as hard as I am to make the ranch successful. What's your answer, Jerry? Do you think you'd like to go into partnership with me and Alison?" she challenged.

He shook his head and smiled crookedly. "It's so insane it just might work, do you know that?"

"That's what I thought!" Edie laughed, unable to check the flow of happiness at his silent agreement.

"We are really going to own a ranch." Alison said it aloud, as if she needed it repeated to believe it.

"We have an awful lot to do," Edie sobered. "First we are going to have to get in touch with a real-estate company to find out what's on the market. We are all agreed on South Dakota, aren't we?"

"How else are we going to have a Dakota dream ranch?" Jerry mocked.

"And we aren't going to jump at the first place that's up for sale, either," she insisted. "We aren't in any hurry, so let's find the right ranch for us, agreed?" Both nodded.

"What about this place?" Jerry wondered.

"We'll sell it," Edie decided. "Burn the bridges. Of course that means the house and barn are going to need a fresh coat of paint. The fences, too."

"We'd better not put it up for sale until we are fairly sure we've found a ranch," Jerry cautioned.

"Yes, otherwise we'll have to find a place to keep our horses until we move," Alison agreed, then asked, "We are taking our horses, aren't we?"

"Definitely." Jerry nodded and glanced questioningly at his half-sister. "Didn't you say that buckskin you bought last winter would make a good roping horse?"

"I think so. Try him out this afternoon and see for yourself," she suggested.

"I'll do that."

Alison rose from her chair. "I'm going to get a paper and pencil so we can make a list of all the things we need to do. This is going to take some organization."

CHAPTER TWO

NEEDLESS TO SAY, the Gibbs family's decision was scoffed at, ridiculed and the butt of many jokes in the area. No one quite believed that they really intended to go through with it.

It wasn't easy to carry out their plan, either. To begin with, there weren't many ranches for sale in the Black Hills region of South Dakota. They were forced to reject those that were available as too costly, too large or too small. But Edie persisted in trying, and with her as their leader, Jerry and Alison followed suit.

The waiting time was not idly spent. The quarter horses Alison had trained for the show ring and speed events were retrained for working use. Two of the five horses had to be sold when they proved too nervous and unsuitable. In addition, Alison completed her horseshoeing course while Edie and Jerry read every available piece of literature regarding ranch management, cattle and land use. Others didn't take their plans seriously, but they did.

Four months from the Sunday they had sat around the table, made their decision and begun their plans, the real-estate agent called to tell

Edie about a ranch that had just been placed on the market.

The owner, an elderly man, was being forced into retirement by an injury. Everything about the ranch sounded ideal, from its total acreage, the amount of pastureland and hay ground, ample water supply, to the financial terms of the sale. Having left Alison behind to look after the horses and the house, Edie and Jerry flew to Rapid City for a first-hand look at the ranch to be certain it was what had been represented to them.

The real-estate agent met them at the airport and drove them out to the property. Snow covered the land, hiding more than it revealed as it followed the curvature of the hills and dipped into gullies. The dark green of pines was scattered across the winter landscape. Driving into the ranch yard, Edie viewed the outbuildings with their snow-covered roofs and drifts banked close to their walls. There was no movement, no sign of stock, but smoke curled out of the chimney of the house to wind a white trail against a startling blue sky.

"The buildings look run-down, don't they?" Jerry observed in a remark to Edie.

"With luck their appearance is deceiving," she replied in a low voice. "They must be structurally sound or they would have collapsed."

The tires crunched in the snow as the real-estate agent slowed the car to a stop in the center of the yard. Switching off the engine, he glanced at them. "Would you like to walk around outside first? Anson Carver, the owner, is on crutches, so we'll have to show ourselves around. The footing is too tricky for him to be hobbling around on."

"We'll look around first," Edie agreed.

She buttoned up her fleece-lined suede parka as Jerry stepped out of the car and pulled his cowboy hat low on his forehead. Edie discovered why he did this when she slid out and a stiff wind blew its icy breath over any exposed skin. Bareheaded, she turned up the fleece collar of her coat and buried her hands in the warm pockets.

They tramped around and through the ranch buildings. As Edie had suspected, the barns and sheds were soundly built, but there were boards and windowpanes that needed replacing. The sliding track for the barn door had broken and another side door was precariously hinged. The signs of repair they did see were the lick-and-a-promise kind. Even the corral and holding pens of the feedlot were constructed out of an assortment of materials—boards, wooden posts, split rails—whatever was handy and the right length at the time.

Trying to hold the front of his topcoat shut against a tugging wind, the agent produced an aerial photograph of the property and oriented them to their location so he could point out boundaries and landmarks. The picture had been taken during the summer, so it was difficult to recognize much with the wild and rolling terrain blanketed with snow.

They wandered farther out from the ranch yard into the near pasture. The snow was nearly to the top of Edie's insulated boots. A thin crust on the top crunched with each step. Jerry paused to sweep away a patch of snow with his boot. Beneath the snow was a tangle of long, yellow grass frozen together in thick clumps. The agent was busy extolling the merits of the place, stressing its wild, natural beauty. It took a few pointed questions from Edie regarding more practical matters, such as how many head of cattle they could expect the land to support, before he realized she would not be swayed into buying a place merely because of its beauty.

When they turned back toward the ranch yard, Edie moved to the fence row where a strip had been drifted clear of snow parallel to the line. She slipped on a patch of ice and grabbed for a post to keep from falling into a drift. Instead of supporting her, the wooden post gave under the pressure of her grasping hand. Jerry's quick reflexes kept her from stumbling to her knees.

"It must have rotted through at the base," he murmured grimly under his breath, and ran a calculating eye along the fence line.

Edie knew what he was thinking. The entire property would probably need new fencing. "This place needs a lot of work."

"You can say that again," Jerry agreed before they caught up with the agent.

The house was in no better repair than the rest of the buildings. It was a one-story, rambling affair that appeared to have had rooms added on with no attempt to adhere to design. White paint was chipped and peeling away to expose gray boards. A knock on the door brought a summons to enter. The interior of the house was as cheerless and dingy as the outside. After the brilliance of the bright sun glaring off white snow outdoors, it took Edie a moment to adjust to the gloom.

The front door had opened directly into a living room where an old wood stove was giving off waves of heat. The sudden change in temperature made Edie's chilled skin tingle with needle-sharp pain. The cold had nipped her cheeks red and made her facial muscles stiff, while the wind had tousled her chestnut hair into casual disorder. She paused inside the door to unbutton her coat and smooth her hair, not wanting to track into the house with her snow-wet boots on. The real-estate agent didn't appear to suffer from any such compunction and walked to a corner of the room where an old man sat in an armchair with one plaster-cast leg propped on a footstool.

"Hello, Mr. Carver. I'm Ned Jenkins from the real-estate office," the agent introduced himself. "I telephoned you this morning to let you know I was bringing these people out to look at your ranch."

"I remember," the old man's gruff voice

answered, then he turned his keenly piercing gaze to the pair standing by the door. He waved an impatient hand for them to enter the living room. "Come in. I don't intend to shout across the room to carry on a conversation with you."

"Let me take off my boots first so I don't track," Edie stated, and bent to unfasten them. A puddle of dirty water was already beginning to form on the floor around her feet.

"Take them off if you've a mind to," the old man scoffed, "but a little water and mud ain't going to be strange to this floor."

Regardless of his lack of concern, Edie went ahead and removed her boots, and Jerry did likewise. She set them neatly against the wall before crossing the room in her stocking-clad feet to meet the present owner.

Aware that Jerry was a step behind her, Edie stopped in front of the old man's chair. Age had wrinkled his sun-browned face and thinned his hair until there were only wispy gray tufts atop his head that he made no attempt to tame into place.

The real-estate agent introduced them. "Mr. Carver, this is Mrs. Gibbs from Illinois. Mr. Anson Carver, the owner of the property."

"How do you do, Mr. Carver?" Edie was faintly surprised by the firmness of the grip of the withered hand that clasped hers.

"This is her son, Jerry Gibbs," the agent continued the introductions.

"How do you do, sir?" The crispness of

Jerry's acknowledgment hinted at the years he'd spent in the military.

"Your son?" Anson Carver's sharp gaze swung back to her, sweeping her from head to foot. "What did you do? Have him when you were straight out of puberty?"

At first Edie was taken aback by the crude and blunt question. Then a rueful smile slanted her mouth. "Jerry is my stepson," she admitted.

"Where's your husband? How come he sent you instead of coming himself?" he demanded with continuing bluntness.

"I lost my husband eight months ago, Mr. Carver. I'm a widow," Edie stated in a voice that invited no sympathy.

Again she was subject to his scrutiny as he took special note of her figure revealed by the unbuttoned parka swinging open. "With a face and a figure like yours, you won't be a widow for long."

After his previous remarks, Edie wasn't shocked by this statement from him. "I believe you are flattering me," she smiled it away.

"At my age I don't have to say things I don't mean. In fact I can say a lot of things I do mean." His smile indicated that he derived tremendous pleasure from doing just that and shocking people in the process. Definitely an irascible rascal, Edie decided. "Pull up a chair and sit down. I'm getting a crick in my neck looking up at you," Anson Carver ordered.

The agent brought a straight chair over for Edie to sit on while Jerry got a chair for himself. It was too hot this close to the heating stove to leave her coat on, so Edie took it off and draped it on the chair back.

"So you came out here to look at my ranch," the older man declared in a gruff challenge. "What do you think of it?"

Edie took a breath then told him. "To be frank, Mr. Carver, you've let it go to hell."

Her candor startled him. With a frown he grumbled, "The place seemed to get too big for me to handle alone. Either that or I got too old. I admit it needs fixing up here and there."

"Here and there?" She lifted a challenging eyebrow. The heavily ribbed, biscuit-colored pullover she was wearing with her brown corduroy slacks gave Edie a very earthy and countryish look. "Your buildings are in need of repair. I doubt if there is a section of fence on the property that doesn't need to be replaced. And who knows what other things the snow is hiding? It's going to take a lot of labor and material to bring this place up to par."

"In other words you think I'm asking too much for the ranch?" he bristled.

"Yes, I do," Edie admitted.

"I suppose your husband left you a bunch of money and you've decided to invest it in a cattle ranch." He sounded faintly contemptuous, but Edie had faced that attitude many times in these months since they'd made their decisions. "Who's gonna run it for you?"

"Nobody is going to run it for us. We are going to do it ourselves," she said, nodding toward Jerry to include him in her plural pronoun.

"Do you think you can handle it?"

"We'll do a better job than you have lately," Edie shrugged.

"You're pretty frisky for such a slip of a gal. If push come to shove, you'd do some shoving yourself, wouldn't you?" he grinned unexpectedly. "What do you think this place is worth?"

Edie told him and added her terms. They haggled back and forth for several minutes. Every time the real-estate agent tried to make a relevant point, the old man told him to shut up. They went through a rapid series of compromises until the last difference in their two positions was settled.

"Lady, you drive a hard bargain, but you just bought yourself a ranch." The man extended his hand to shake on the deal. He sliced a piercing look at the agent. "Did you make a note of all the terms so we can draw up an agreement?"

"Yes, sir. I—"

"Fine. Start writing it up." Anson Carver was quick to dismiss him from the conversation. Now he was directing his attention to Jerry. "You look like you got a head on your shoulders, boy. Do you think you and your stepmomma can handle this place?"

"I do or I wouldn't be here," Jerry stated with a faint smile.

"Got any more like him?" Anson Carver shot the question at Edie.

"I have a daughter. She's looking after our place in Illinois while we're here."

He rested his head against the chair back for a moment. "I'm glad someone like you is buying the ranch. I didn't want to see it gobbled up into somebody else's holdings," he explained rather absently. "I've lived in this house seventy-two years. It's good to know that somebody will be living in it when I'm gone."

"Where will you go, Mr. Carver?" Edie asked.

He pursed his lips, puckering them as if there was a bad taste in his mouth. "I'm moving to my granddaughter's in Deadwood. She's got a room all fixed up for me, she says."

"You'll always be welcome to stop by," Edie stated.

His gaze swung to her, a sudden twinkle lighting his eyes with mischief. "A widow and two kids," he chortled in apparent delight. "I'd love to see his face when he finds out!"

"Whose face?" A frown flickered across her forehead.

"It's a private joke." He didn't explain. "You won't understand until after you've lived here for a while. At my age there are few pleasures left in life that I can enjoy. But to know that I'm the one to show the he-bull in these parts that he can't have everything the way he wants it gives me a lot of satisfaction. Mind you, it's nothing personal, but I'll have many a laugh over this in that room in Deadwood."

"Does it have something to do with the ranch?" Edie persisted, puzzled by his answer and certain that he intended her to be.

"You aren't going to have any problems you can't handle," he assured her. "When do you want possession?"

Edie glanced at Jerry. There were a great many things that had to be done in Illinois—put their house and acreage up for sale and pack. Plus there was all the legal paperwork involved in buying this place.

"The end of March? What do you think?" she asked.

"That sounds good to me," Jerry nodded. "Spring will be breaking. That gives us a little over two months."

"Would that suit you, Mr. Carver?" she asked.

"Fine. Make a note of that, Jenkins," he ordered. "While he's writing all this down, why don't you go in the kitchen, Mrs. Gibbs, and fix us some coffee? I would, but—" he thumped the plaster cast on his leg "—I don't get around too good." He pointed to a hallway behind him. "It's that way."

"I don't mind at all," Edie agreed, and rose from her chair.

As she left the room she heard Jerry ask,

"When we were walking around outside, I didn't see any sign of livestock. Don't you have any?"

"No. When I got laid up, I didn't have any way of looking after them. And I never could keep good help on the place. So I asked...my neighbor to round up anything that moved and sell it."

Edie couldn't help thinking it was comforting to know they would have the kind of neighbors who were willing to help out in time of need.

EVERYTHING SEEMED TO FALL INTO PLACE after that. Within a month after they had listed their Illinois property for sale they had a buyer. All the legal paperwork for both the sale of their property and the purchase of the ranch was completed in two months. During the last week there was a string of farewell parties for them.

Edie was aware that many people thought she was being disrespectful to Joe's memory by selling the place where they had lived and moving away. But Joe had made this chance possible. She was convinced it would be a greater injustice to him if she didn't take it.

Happy seemed an inadequate description of the way she felt. She was excited, eager, looking forward to this new life and its challenges. It seemed an adventure. She wanted to laugh aloud for no reason at all. Since she was alone in the cab of the rented U-haul truck, she did.

A series of signs were tacked to the row of

fence posts along the highway. Edie read them
with quick glances and reached for the mike of
the CB radio, temporarily mounted on the dash.
It had been one of the going-away presents.

"Breaker one-nine. This is the Dakota
Dreamer in the rocking chair. How about that
Pony Girl up there at my front door?" She used
the C.B. radio jargon to call Alison in the car
ahead of the truck.

"You've got the Pony Girl. Come back,"
Alison responded.

"Did you read those signs we just passed?
Come back."

"I must have missed them. What did they say
this time?" her daughter asked.

"They said, 'You are entering God's country.
Don't drive through it like hell,'" Edie told her.

"Yeah, so ease back on the hammer, Pony
Girl," Jerry joined their radio conversation.
"Your back door has a load of dogmeat, in case
you've forgotten. Slow it down." He was bringing up the rear of their small caravan in his
pickup truck, pulling the horse trailer loaded
with their horses and gear.

"My foot got heavy, Leatherneck. I'm easing
it back," Alison replied.

"Hey, Pony Girl," Jerry called her back. "If
you see a rest area, pull over. I want to check the
horses."

"That's a ten-four," Alison agreed.

Then the radio went silent for a while in
Edie's cab except for the chatter of some other

CBers some distance away. Her gaze strayed to the rolling landscape of the South Dakota prairie. Its flat appearance was deceptive as its grassed sod undulated toward the horizon. Trees, mostly cottonwoods, clustered wherever there was water. There was a timeless quality about this open expanse of land stretching endlessly into the beyond that had a magic all its own. Patches of snow could be seen in shadowed ditches, an indication that winter hadn't released its grip on the land.

After traveling almost a full hour, Edie saw the dark mass looming on the horizon. Her mouth barely curved as she recognized it, her pulse quickening in a surge of excitement. Again she reached for the CB mike to share her discovery with Alison and Jerry.

"Breaker one-nine for that Pony Girl and Leatherneck. Do you see that on the horizon?" she asked.

"Where?" Alison came back. "You mean that mass of clouds? I hope we aren't in for a storm."

"Those aren't clouds," Jerry corrected. "That's the Black Hills. Now you know how they got their names."

"There's some roadside tables just ahead. It looks as if there's room for all of us to park," Alison informed them. Edie saw the turning indicator blinking on the car ahead of her and flipped hers on.

When the rental van filled with their furniture

and belongings was parked and the motor
switched off, Edie grabbed her parka and the
thermos of coffee from the passenger seat.
Alison was already standing by the roadside picnic table, stretching and arching muscles
cramped from long hours of driving. Yesterday
they had started out at daybreak and continued
till dark, crossing from Iowa into Nebraska.
Now the Black Hills dominated the horizon, rising above the prairie—pine-covered slopes giving the deceptive impression of darkness and
earning the landmark its name. Their ranch,
their new home, was on the western edge of this
sacred Indian land within the national forest.

"We don't have far to go now," Edie
declared as she joined Alison by the picnic table.
A cold wind tried to slide its icy fingers inside
the collar of her jacket, but Edie fastened the
top button to keep it out.

"Mmm, coffee." Alison took one of the cups
and held it while Edie filled it half-full. "I wish I
could have gone with you guys to see the
ranch."

"Don't be expecting too much," Edie cautioned. "The place is run-down and needs a lot
of work to put it in shape."

"I hope there is enough coffee there for me."
Jerry paused beside her, wearing an insulated
vest over his plaid flannel shirt, but otherwise
coatless. He rubbed his hands together to warm
them as Edie poured him half a cup of coffee,
too. "The ranch may not look like much, but we

know for sure it isn't worthless," he said, picking up the conversation where Edie had left off.

"What?" At first Edie didn't follow his meaning. Then she remembered with a nod of her head. "You mean that offer."

"Yes." He sipped at the hot coffee. "We could have sold the place for a handsome profit even before we'd signed the final papers to buy it."

"Maybe we should have," Alison suggested.

"Where would we have gone?" Edie reasoned. "Our place was already sold. We had to move. Who knows how long it might have taken us to find another ranch so ideally suited. Can you imagine how much it would have cost if we'd had to pay to board our horses?"

"I suppose you're right," her daughter conceded.

Edie knew why her daughter was having doubts. The answer was simple—Craig Gurney. He had managed to turn up at every farewell party given for them. It was to Alison's credit that she had treated him coolly in the beginning, but Craig's persistence had her weakening toward the end.

"Speaking of horses—" Jerry paused to drain the last of the coffee from his cup and hand it back to Edie "—I'd better check on them."

Edie watched him for a second then turned, a light of anticipation glittering in her eyes. Tomorrow they would be riding the horses on their very own ranch, exploring the property. Her mouth opened to share the thought with Alison until she saw the wistful, faraway look in her daughter's eyes as she looked back at the road they had traveled.

"Are you sorry we left, Alison?" Edie asked gently.

It was a full second before Alison blinked and let her gaze refocus. "I . . ." she began uncertainly, then finished with a sighing, "No."

Masking her relief, Edie offered, "More coffee? There's only a little bit left in the thermos."

Alison held out her cup in silent acceptance. "Mom, were you a virgin when you married dad?" she asked thoughtfully.

Craig Gurney had to be responsible for that question, Edie thought as she replied, "Yes."

"You didn't . . . anticipate your wedding or anything like that, did you?" Alison persisted.

"No." A smile twitched at the corners of Edie's mouth, hinting at a pair of dimples. "But it isn't easy to anticipate anything when you have a five-year-old boy along as chaperon on all your dates."

While taking a sip of coffee, Alison was overcome by a laugh. She choked and sputtered, and coughed out the laugh. "I'm sorry." Her eyes were brimming with tears and shining with laughter. "But for a second I was trying to visualize dad sweeping you off your feet. And he just wasn't the type," she declared in a voice that bubbled with her amusement. "I can't see dad ever tempting any woman into a sinful situation. Maybe a daughter can't visualize her father as a lover."

"Probably not," Edie agreed, smiling with her daughter, knowing Alison wasn't criticizing Joe.

"Dad was good-looking in his own way," Alison recalled. "But he was never an exciting kind of man. I don't mean he was dull. I used to get so exasperated with him when he'd forget your birthday that I wanted to bat him over the head. One time I told him that instead of kissing you on the cheek when he came home, he should take you in his arms and do it properly. Of course he didn't take my advice," she sighed in a gentle way to indicate it hadn't mattered.

"Joe wasn't very demonstrative, but he was a good man—the best." There was a tiny catch in Edie's voice. While he hadn't been a passionate man, he had made her feel good—needed, wanted and loved.

"You miss him, too, don't you, mom?" Alison offered in commiseration.

"Yes. It isn't so bad during the day because he was usually at work. In the evenings he was usually in his workshop. But when I wake up in the night and he isn't there to cuddle up to, that's when I really miss him," Edie admitted softly, staring into her empty cup.

"Do you think you'll get married again, mom?"

The question jerked her chin up. After a

startled second had passed, Edie emitted an incredulous and breathless laugh. "Your father hasn't even been dead a year. I'm certainly not looking for a replacement."

"But if you meet someone," Alison persisted.

"If I met a man that I thought I could love and who could love me, I would consider it." What else could she say? She certainly wasn't going to pretend she was blind to the possibility it might happen. Her life certainly wasn't going to come to an end if it didn't.

"They say that every man makes love differently, that just because you've been to bed with with one man doesn't mean the feeling will be the same with the next. It has to do with the two chemistries involved, I guess," Alison volunteered absently.

"*They* say that, do they?" Edie mocked, amused by the "voice of experience" talking. "I'm afraid I wouldn't know about that."

"Oh, mom!" Alison blushed and laughed.

Edie joined in. "I hope you don't object if I don't bother to check *their* theory to see if it's true or not."

"I'll disown you if you do," Alison continued to laugh.

"Hey! Come on, you two!" Jerry shouted from his truck. "Let's get on the road. We still have a way to go and a lot of unloading to do before nightfall."

"We'll be right there!" Alison called back, and handed the plastic coffee cup to Edie. "I think he's trying to tell us to hurry up," she grinned.

"You could be right." Edie stacked the cups inside one another and screwed them onto the thermos.

Jerry was in his truck with the motor running by the time Edie crawled into the cab of the rental van. She warmed up the engine and waited until Alison had pulled onto the highway before falling in behind the car. Jerry was right. They did have a way to go, and the last stretch would be on graveled roads.

CHAPTER THREE

STOPPED IN THE RANCH YARD, the three of them were slow to step out of their individual vehicles. When they did, they gravitated toward each other, unconsciously solidifying into a united front.

"It looks worse, doesn't it?" Edie murmured.

Without the pristine whiteness of snow cover, the run-down condition of the ranch stood out against its stark background of brown grass and craggy hills with shaggy clusters of pines. The buildings were weathered and gray, the patchwork repairs telling their own tales of shoddy workmanship. The corral behind the barn looked incapable of holding a newborn calf. The house had four different colors of shingles on its roof.

"This is it?" Alison's skeptical expression revealed her opinion.

"I warned you that it needed work," Edie reminded her.

"I thought you meant a face-lift, not major surgery," she replied with faint disgust.

"The first thing we *have* to do is fix that corral, so we have somewhere to unload the horses," Jerry stated with his usual practicality.

Glancing at the sun dipping toward the western horizon, Edie added, "We'd better all help if we want it done before dark."

They practically rebuilt the corral before they were finished—replacing this post, bracing another, ripping out rotting boards and tearing barn stalls apart for replacement boards. When they were finished it was almost twilight. The end result didn't look any more attractive than the previous corral, but they knew it was sturdy.

The temperature was dropping with the setting of the sun. Although the hard labor had all three of them perspiring, Edie felt the clammy chill setting in. Jerry was maneuvering the horse trailer into position to unload with instructions from Alison. Edie glanced toward the bleak exterior of the house and the soot-blackened chimney on its roof.

"You two unload the horses. I'll see what I can do about getting a fire started in the house," she said, and received an acknowledging wave from Jerry.

Without the clutter of Anson Carver's worn furniture, the interior of the house was more depressing than the exterior. The cold, dreary emptiness of the rooms was not welcoming. To make matters worse, when Edie flipped the light switch to chase away the gathering shadows, nothing happened. It was the same with every light switch in the house, which meant they had no electricity. Evidently the power company had not carried out their instructions.

Sighing, Edie walked back outside to the rental van for the battery-operated flashlight. Somewhere, packed neatly away in boxes, there were candles and a hurricane lamp. With her luck, Edie was positive they would be in the last box she searched.

The beam of the flashlight gave off enough illumination for her to check the wood stove to be certain the damper was open before she lighted it. When the fire was blazing strongly, she left the living room to check out the rest of the house. What she found made her spirits droop even lower and reminded her of Anson Carver's comment that his house had known dirt intimately. Cobwebs, dust and dirt coated everything. And this was her new beginning on her dream ranch. Her mouth twisted in irony.

The front door opened and she heard two pairs of footsteps stomp wearily into the house. "I'm starving," Alison mumbled. The comment was followed immediately by, "Mom? What's the matter with the lights?"

She stepped into the hallway to flash the beam toward them. "We don't have any electricity. There must have been a mix-up."

"Oh, good grief!" her daughter exclaimed in disgust. "Now we'll have to stumble around in the dark to unload everything. What about something to eat?"

"We'll probably have to settle for cold sandwiches," Edie admitted in a sigh.

"Do you want me to bring in the ice chest and groceries from the truck?" Jerry asked.

"Yes, and all the cleaning supplies, too," she added.

As Alison walked down the hallway illuminated by the flashlight beam, she ran into a cobweb. "Ugh!" She wiped it off her face with an expressive grimace of distaste. "This place is filthy!"

"Yes," Edie agreed. "I'm afraid all we're going to accomplish tonight is scrubbing out the bedrooms so we'll have a place to sleep."

It was nearly midnight before all three bedrooms were cleaned, the bedroom furniture unloaded from the van and the beds made. Alison unearthed the candles and kerosene lantern, which helped. They were not only without electricity, but also without hot water. None of them relished a cold shower no matter how dirty they were, so Edie warmed a pail of water on the wood stove. They washed the worst of the dirt off and tumbled into their beds too exhausted to care.

The next morning they unloaded the rest of the furniture from the van. Edie left Alison and Jerry at the ranch to finish cleaning the house and arranging their belongings while she drove the rented truck into town to return it and find out what the problem was with the electricity. She expected to be finished by noon and made arrangements with Jerry to pick her up at the grocery store.

It was almost three o'clock before she met him. What groceries they had needed he had already bought and stacked in the front seat of the cab.

"I was beginning to wonder what had happened to you." Jerry took one look at her seething expression and tried to hide a grin. "I don't think I'll ask what kept you."

"I've been getting the royal runaround," she snapped and crawled into the cab of his truck, pushing the grocery sacks out of her way and still fuming. "I kept getting shoved from one person at the power company to another. First they tried to tell me that we hadn't requested service."

"Did you show them a copy of the letter we sent?" Jerry started the motor and reversed away from the curb into the street.

"Yes." Edie glared out the window at the boardwalks shaded by jutting overhangs of western-styled buildings. "Then they tried to tell me we hadn't made a deposit. I have never been anyplace where people were so incredibly ignorant and uncooperative!"

"Did you get it straightened out?"

"Finally. We are supposed to have the electricity connected late this afternoon." She leaned back in her seat, rubbing her forehead where it was pounding.

"Should we hold our breath?" Jerry teased.

"They'd better have it turned on. I want a shower tonight." She closed her eyes and tried to will away the angry tension. "How is everything going at the ranch?"

"Okay. I left Alison cleaning the kitchen... and swearing," he answered.

Edie opened one eye to look at him, an impish light dancing in the hazel depths. "I hope she has it finished before we get back so we don't have to help."

"Right!" Jerry tipped his head back to laugh in hearty agreement. "My hands are starting to look all funny and pink from all that detergent water."

Edie closed her eyes again and let the rhythm of the rolling wheels on the pavement soothe her into relaxing. When Jerry made the turn onto the graveled road, she opened them to study the scenery racing by the pickup window. Tall ponderosa pines hugged the edges of the road to form a green corridor. Here and there they thinned out to make a meadow of yellow grass. The winding gravel road alternated between sun and shadow. Beyond the pine branches there were glimpses of high mountains, granite rock interlacing with trees. A valley opened up, grassy and serene.

"Even with all the unexpected problems, I'm glad we're here," Edie murmured.

"So am I. None of us thought it was going to be easy. But we know all about work." Jerry slid her a smile. "We never have been afraid of it, and we have more reason than ever not to be now.''

''That's true,'' she laughed softly. They had a ranch to build and a future.

''Tomorrow we'll have to ride the perimeters and check the fences.''

For the rest of the drive they talked of the things that needed to be done to prepare for the purchase of stock cattle as well as some yearling calves for fall sale. When they arrived at the ranch, Alison met them at the door, demanding to know where they had been. Edie and Jerry exchanged a silent look of humor. They knew Alison was disgruntled because she had been left to finish the cleaning alone, and they knew how much she detested housework. As Edie was relating her tale of battle with the power company, the lights came on. Alison forgot her ill temper to join in the cheers for Edie's triumph over the utility company's red-tape foul-up.

With the house in some semblance of order and as sparkling clean as the dingy place could ever be, the three went out to briefly exercise the horses, then brushed them down and grained them for the night. At six-thirty they sat down for the first home-cooked meal they had had in three days.

''Did you hear a car door slam?'' Alison asked and cocked her head to listen before helping herself to a second portion of macaroni and cheese.

''If you turned that radio down a notch we

might be able to hear ourselves think," Jerry suggested dryly.

"It isn't that loud," she protested, but reached behind her to turn down the volume of the radio on the kitchen counter.

Instantly there was a loud knock at the front door. Edie frowned in surprise and started to get up. "Who could that be?"

"I'll answer it." Jerry waved her into her seat. "It's probably that real-estate agent checking to see how we've settled in. Wasn't his name Jenkins?"

"I think so," Edie agreed as he left the room. The lights flickered overhead and her mouth thinned into an angry line. "Or maybe it's somebody with the utility company. I'd better go to the door, too."

She emerged from the kitchen as Jerry opened the front door. Edie could tell by the reserved tone of his greeting that her stepson didn't know the person calling.

A pleasantly deep male voice responded, "Good evening. I would like to speak with Mrs. Gibbs if she's free."

There was an impersonal quality to the request, yet it carried the crispness of authority. Edie noticed the way Jerry unconsciously squared his shoulders and stood a little straighter, as if he was facing a commanding officer.

"If you'll step inside, I'll call her." Jerry swung the door wide to admit the man. As he pivoted, he saw her in the hall. "Edie, there's a man here to see you."

Curious, she moved forward. The man was tall, over six feet. She knew that because he had to remove his hat and duck his head to walk through the front door. He was wearing a tailored leather jacket that emphasized the breadth of his shoulders and the relative slimness of his hips. Western-cut brown trousers flared slightly over his boots.

Her first impression of the stranger reminded her of a range bull, all leashed power and raw virility. This power and virility were repeated in the way he carried himself with an aloof nobility. He held dominion over his kind and it showed. Members of this proud, rugged breed were dangerous when riled and implacable in the face of danger. Even the most powerful predators would veer away from this range bull.

And Edie found herself treading warily in his presence. When her gaze skimmed his hard-hewn features, there was nothing in the thrusting power of his jaw and chin, the slightly crooked bend of his nose or the firmly cut line of his mouth to change her initial impression. The flecks of iron in his shaggy dark brown hair was a sign not of encroaching weakness, but of maturity, of a man in his prime. Or maybe her opinion had been influenced by the hardness of the iron-gray eyes that took note of her approach.

Her smile was pleasant enough when she

stopped in front of him. It was only natural, Edie supposed, to feel intimidated by his size. She also understood why Jerry had felt the impulse to snap to attention, but she suppressed it. Here she was the one in charge. The fact remained that, although this stranger was standing in her living room with his hat in his hand, there was nothing humble about him.

"I am Edie Gibbs," she confirmed her identity. "You wanted to see me?"

The mocking glint that flashed in his eyes gave Edie the impression that he was mentally quirking an eyebrow at the information, although there wasn't a flicker of any such movement. His gaze started at the top of her head and slowly worked its way down.

First Edie realized that she hadn't combed her hair since coming into the house from exercising and caring for the horses. The soft, curling length of her golden brown hair was undoubtedly windblown and tousled. His inspection of her face made her conscious that she wore no makeup; even her lipstick had worn off at the supper table. It took every ounce of willpower not to moisten her lips when he studied their contours.

His silent appraisal continued its downward progress, reminding her of the boy's flannel shirt she wore, a size too small. In consequence the plaid material was stretched tautly across the rounded fullness of her breasts, the buttoned front gaping slightly. It wasn't a stripping look.

A man like this knew what was underneath without needing to mentally disrobe a woman to get his kicks. Edie didn't know how she knew that, but she did. Yet it didn't make her feel any less uncomfortable.

Then his gaze was skimming her faded denims, hugging tightly to her slim hips and shapely thighs before running stovepipe straight to her boots. He even took note of the scuffed and weathered leather of her boots, permanently stained with mud and manure.

When his metallic smooth gaze returned to her face, the tour of inspection hadn't taken more than twenty seconds, but it had seemed an eternity of irritating discomfort to Edie. The words burned on the tip of her tongue to inform him that she hadn't been expecting visitors—and he should have expected to find her still in work clothes from doing ranch chores. Edie held them back because she wasn't about to defend the way she dressed in her own home—not to a complete stranger.

"*You* are the widow Gibbs?" The inflection in the husky timbre of his voice smoothly demanded verification.

It had been an exasperating day. Irritation again raced through nerve ends that had only begun to recover. His implication that she didn't fit the image of a middle-aged widow set her teeth on edge. Admittedly she was on the wrong side of thirty, but it didn't mean she had to be dumpy and plain or clad in black with smelling salts at hand.

"Yes, I am." The faint note of belligerence in her answer didn't appear to register in his expression. She lifted her chin to an angle of controlled challenge as her smile lost its warmth. "You have the advantage. You know who I am, but I don't know who you are."

"Will Maddock." He didn't extend his hand in greeting. "I own the Diamond D Ranch."

Edie guessed she was supposed to be impressed, but since she had never heard of it—or him—she simply filed the information away in her mind.

"The Diamond D?" Jerry spoke up. He had been standing to one side. "I saw that brand on some cattle on my way into town this noon. They were in a pasture next to our property."

At the sound of Jerry's voice, Will Maddock had turned his head to subject her stepson to his appraisal. He measured Jerry with a practiced eye, noting his lanky but solidly muscled frame and the shadow of a man's beard on his cheek, not the peach fuzz of a boy.

"You own the land next to ours?" Jerry questioned.

"Yes." It was a simple, straightforward answer.

"Then you are our neighbor," Edie realized.

The iron-hard gaze swung lazily back to her. "Yes."

She stifled the resentment that she had begun to form against him. Will Maddock was obviously calling to welcome them to the area, a gesture of polite friendliness that shouldn't be slapped away simply because she had had a bad day and was therefore quicker to take exception. Possibly Will Maddock was the same neighbor who had rounded up and sold Anson Carver's livestock when he was laid up. He struck her as the kind of man whom you would want on your side if you were in trouble. She definitely wouldn't want him as an enemy.

"It's a pleasure to meet you, Mr. Maddock." She extended her hand in belated greeting.

He glanced at it, hesitated then accepted the gesture. When his work-roughened hand closed around hers, Edie experienced a tremor of surprise. She had always thought Joe's hands were large, but her hand looked like a child's against Will Maddock's. It was such a strong, capable hand, it didn't need to assert its strength by crushing her fingers. There was the firm warmth of its clasp, then her hand was released. A little overwhelmed by the discovery, Edie didn't notice that Will Maddock hadn't returned her phrase, nor one like it.

Instead she turned to introduce Jerry and caught sight of Alison, who had slipped unnoticed into the room. "This is my stepson, Jerry Gibbs, and my daughter, Alison. Mr. Will Maddock."

Jerry stepped forward to shake hands with

him, but Alison simply smiled and nodded from across the room. It was part of her natural reserve when meeting strangers, but not caused by shyness.

Remembering her manners, Edie invited, "Won't you sit down, Mr. Maddock? Let me take your coat."

He accepted the invitation to have a seat but refused the second suggestion. "No, I won't be staying long."

He did unbutton the leather jacket to let it swing open before sitting in the armchair that had always been Joe's favorite. But Edie never remembered Joe ever filling it the way this man did. In fact, it took on the appearance of a throne. Again there was that little flicker of resentment that Edie had to suppress.

"We had just finished supper and were about to have some coffee when you arrived." She told the white lie out of a sense of courtesy. "Would you like a cup?"

"No." His iron-flat gaze made a pointed glance toward Jerry and Alison. "I would like to speak to you in private, if I may."

The skin along the back of her neck prickled, irritated by the polite phrasing that didn't disguise his order for them to leave. His whole attitude left Edie with the feeling that he belonged here and she didn't, that his orders were to be obeyed as a matter of course.

"Speak to me in regards to what, Mr. Maddock?" she challenged, and sat down on the

flowered sofa, leaning against the cushions to
indicate that she was the one in her own home.

"This ranch."

"This is a family holding, Mr. Maddock,"
Edie informed him. "Alison and Jerry are directly involved in all phases of it. There is no
need for them to leave. In fact, since it's the
ranch you want to talk about, they definitely
should stay."

Briefly she wondered what he wanted to talk
about. There had been no mention of a boundary dispute. Perhaps he had a complaint to
make.

"A few weeks ago I made you an offer for
this ranch," he began.

"You made the offer?" she repeated. "We
did receive an offer on the property, but we
didn't bother to inquire who made it since we
weren't interested in selling it."

"I was told by the real-estate agent that you
had turned it down, even though it meant a
quick and handsome profit," Maddock admitted. "I'm here to raise my offer by fifty dollars
an acre."

Edie raised an eyebrow in surprise, then
glanced at Jerry and Alison who were expressing
a similar reaction of astonishment. "You are
very generous, Mr. Maddock, but we aren't interested in selling it."

Impatience hardened his features. "Let's not
waste time, Mrs. Gibbs. Simply tell me how
much you want."

If there had been any temptation to consider his offer before, it was gone now. "I told you, we aren't interested in selling."

"Everyone has a price," he replied bluntly. "You can use the money to buy a ranch somewhere else—one that isn't as run-down as this one."

"Considering its condition, you seem to want the ranch very badly," she murmured.

"It joins my land," he stated as if that was sufficient reason.

"Do you plan to own every ranch that joins your land, Mr. Maddock? That would seem to be a never-ending goal," she taunted.

His hard gray eyes turned to cold steel. "It took years of neglect and abuse to let this place get in its present condition. I don't intend to stand idly by and let it go from bad to worse while a trio of greenhorns amuse themselves by playing cowboy."

Incensed by his swift condemnation of them without giving them even the smallest chance to prove they might be capable of running a ranch, Edie rose from the sofa. When Will Maddock stood up to face her, she felt like a banty hen tackling a silver-tipped grizzly.

"I suggest, Mr. Maddock, that you don't know us. You haven't even bothered to inquire what our qualifications or experience might be, although it isn't any of your business." She was controlling her temper with an effort, speaking sharply and concisely.

"I know how much work it's going to take to whip this place into shape again."

"We aren't allergic to work. In fact, we have been on a very intimate basis with it all our lives," Edie stated as Jerry and Alison moved over to stand beside her, uniting again.

"There is a lot of back-breaking labor involved, long hours of hard, physical labor. I have no doubt the boy will do his share, or try. But two females?" His gaze flicked over them in obvious contempt for their contribution.

"You are underestimating us," Edie insisted tightly.

His arm moved. Before she could guess his intention, her hand was trapped in his paw. He twisted it upward in front of her face.

"Take a good look at your hands, Mrs. Gibbs, because a month from now you won't recognize them," he told her. "Your fingernails will all be chipped and short. There will be calluses on those smooth palms. Your hands will be as rough as sandpaper. You'll be too exhausted to eat and too tired to sleep. And that's just the beginning!"

"We aren't made of glass." She strained against his grip, but didn't struggle to free herself.

"You'll break." There was a hard sureness in his voice as he released her hand. A numbness tingled through it as circulation was restored.

"Don't be too sure, Mr. Maddock," Edie replied, and refrained from rubbing her hand, not wanting to show any weakness in front of him.

It was a cruel smile that slanted his mouth. "I'm sure of one thing, Mrs. Gibbs—one way or another you are going to sell to me before the year is out."

"That sounds like a threat." She tipped her head back to challenge the man towering in front of her.

"I don't waste time with threats. You aren't hurting anyone but yourself by being stubborn, Mrs. Gibbs." He put his hat on and pulled it low on his forehead. "Let me know what you want for the ranch when you're ready to sell."

He started toward the door. After a second Edie followed him. "It's a pity that you didn't buy the place from Mr. Carver since you want it so much."

Pausing with his hand on the doorknob, he gave her a sidelong look that was shadowed by the brim of his hat. "I was out of the States when he put it on the market, otherwise you wouldn't be here."

He left without a good-evening—just as he had come without a hello. At the sound of an engine starting up, Edie's knees began shaking. She hadn't realized how emotionally tense she had been. It was like shock setting in after the danger had passed.

"I'd sell this ranch to the devil before I'd sell it to him!" Alison declared.

"We aren't selling." Edie whirled to correct that thought. "Not to him. Not to anyone."

"That's who Anson Carver was talking about," Jerry mused, staring thoughtfully in the direction of the car.

"When?" Edie demanded.

"When he said the 'he-bull' wasn't going to get what he wanted," he answered with a faint smile deepening the corners of his mouth. "I'll bet you Maddock tried to buy this place from Carver half a dozen times and Carver wouldn't sell."

"Why wouldn't he sell?" Alison frowned. "Obviously that man Maddock would have paid more money for the ranch. Look what he's offered us!"

"I don't know. Carver mentioned a couple of things," Jerry remembered. "He didn't want the ranch gobbled up in a bigger one, which Maddock's obviously is. And he was glad we were going to be living in this house. Maddock would probably have torn it down or abandoned it."

"You could be right," Edie murmured. The old man had been a cantankerous, stubborn man. She doubted that he had sold the ranch because he needed the money, so his decision to sell to them might not have been dictated by price.

"This house is a dump and an eyesore. I don't blame Maddock if he wanted to tear it down. I wish we could," Alison muttered.

"In time we can fix it up," Edie sighed, because she couldn't agree with her daughter more. "But we have a lot more important things to do first. As Maddock would be quick to remind us if he was here," she finished on a bitter note.

"You've had a rough day, Edie. Why don't you go take a shower and relax?" Jerry suggested.

"What about me?" Alison protested. "This Cinderella hasn't exactly been idle!"

"Turn the radio on and prop your feet up. I'll do the dishes," Jerry volunteered. "According to Maddock, our hands are going to look alike anyway, so I'll give yours a break tonight."

His remark teased an unwilling laugh from Edie and Alison, letting some of their normal good humor return. It helped dispel the doubts Maddock's gloomy predictions had cast.

"Nothing is very bad if we can laugh at it," Alison stated, and they agreed with her.

CHAPTER FOUR

THE NEXT MORNING they were up with the sun. After packing some sandwiches for lunch and a thermos of coffee, the three saddled up their horses and rode out to inspect the property and its boundaries.

The tour around the perimeter of their ranch took the biggest share of the day. They made two discoveries, one of which Edie had already suspected. There wasn't a section of fence line that didn't need to be repaired or replaced.

It was the second discovery that came as a surprise. Their ranch was bounded on three sides by Diamond D land. Maddock's ranch practically surrounded theirs. There was a stark contrast between his neat, precise fence rows running at right angles to the drooping and tumbledown excuse of their fences. Their meadows abounded with thistles while his were thick with nutritious grasses.

None of them mentioned the obvious differences nor acknowledged that Maddock had cause to regard the ranch as a plague on his own. Neither did they admit that there was more work to be done than they had imagined.

That night it was decided that Jerry would go into town the next morning and order the barbed wire and new fence posts while Edie and Alison explored the interior of the ranch property. They needed to learn where the best grazing lands and their water sources were.

No matter how much riding Edie had done in the past, none of it had prepared her bones and muscles for an entire day and part of a second in the saddle. By midday she was so stiff and sore she wanted to cry. There was small consolation in knowing that Alison was suffering, too.

These Dakota hills bore no resemblance to the Illinois landscape where they had ridden before. Here there were deep ravines to be descended and climbed, the horses plunging and rearing to claw their way up, rocky slopes to be negotiated, the horses' iron shoes slipping and stumbling over stones and clear, cold streams to be crossed, the horses splashing the icy water onto their legs. Seldom was there time to admire the view. Daydreaming was usually punished by a low-hanging limb that the unwary rider didn't see in time to duck.

One such branch tried to decapitate Edie. "Damn!" she swore under her breath as her hat was knocked off.

"Are you playing at cowboy?" Alison teased and leaned way over to pick up the hat without dismounting from the black mare.

"If you want me to laugh, use words other

than Maddock's," Edie retorted with a weary grin.

"I'll remember that," Alison laughed, and returned her mother's hat. They had ridden almost to the crest of a ridge. Alison reined her mare in a half circle to traverse the last few yards. "Mom, look!" She pointed toward the valley below. "There's cattle down there. Do you see them?"

When they rode down to investigate they discovered a dozen head of Hereford cattle grazing in the tall grass of a meadow. The Diamond D brand was burned on their rusty red hips.

"What do you suppose they're doing here?" Alison asked.

"Eating our grass," Edie retorted and sighed. "They probably wandered through a break in the fence. We'd better drive them back."

"Our first cattle drive...and it's somebody else's cattle." Alison sent her a laughing glance. "Too bad Jerry isn't here. We could outnumber them."

Herding the cattle back to the boundary fence was a welcome change of pace. After an initial reluctance to leave the lush grass of the meadow, the cattle allowed themselves to be driven back to their home range. There were so many breaks in the fence Edie couldn't guess which one they had come through, so it didn't matter which one they went back through. On the other side they urged the cattle into a trot to chase them away from the fence, then turned and rode back toward the fence.

"Oh, oh," Alison murmured. "It looks like we are about to be caught trespassing."

Edie looked beyond her daughter to see two riders approaching them. Will Maddock was one of them. No one could fail to recognize that muscular frame mounted on a rangy mouse-gray buckskin. The second rider was a girl, a wand-slim rider on a spirited sorrel with a blaze and four white stockings. Edie refused to hurry her bay gelding to reach their own land before Maddock intercepted them. They had a perfectly legitimate reason for trespassing on his property. A few yards short of the fence the four riders reined their horses in to meet.

"Good afternoon, Mr. Maddock," Edie greeted him coolly.

He acknowledged the greeting with a faint nod, but didn't respond in a similar vein. There was nothing in his steady regard to make her so aware of her unflattering masculine clothes. Edie decided the sensation was aroused because he was so damned male that she was automatically conscious of her own sex.

Her gaze broke away from his to study the girl on the prancing, restless sorrel. She looked to be the same age as Alison, but considerably more self-possessed. Hatless, she had a thick mane of brunette hair, long and curling, and her eyes were an arrogant blue.

"This is my daughter, Felicia. Mrs. Gibbs

and her daughter, Alison.'' Will Maddock made the introduction.

"Hello, Felicia." Edie acknowledged the introduction and Alison echoed it. Like her father, Felicia Maddock simply nodded in response. Edie doubted if she was wrong to suspect that his daughter was a spoiled snob.

"Some of your cattle strayed onto our property. We herded them back," Edie explained.

"What can you expect? There isn't anything to stop them," Maddock replied in a dry dismissal of the effectiveness of the dividing fence.

"I am aware of that," Edie countered stiffly.

"Good. Because it's your fence and your problem." He was stating facts, neither taunting nor mocking, just smoothly pointing out where the responsibility rested.

And it was all the more infuriating. "It will soon be remedied." She was rigid.

"Let's go, dad," his daughter urged with undisguised boredom for the conversation taking place. "You promised we would go swimming when we got back," she reminded him, and explained to Alison with an upper-crust dryness, "We have a heated pool."

Will Maddock's response was to tighten the grip on the reins. The big, blue gray buckskin he was riding showed how well-trained it was by backing up in double-quick time and stopping the second the pressure on the bit was eased.

"You're looking tired after only two days,

Mrs. Gibbs," he observed. "You should get some rest." His gloved hand touched the brim of his hat in a farewell gesture before he glanced at his daughter and reined his mount away.

As cantering hooves drummed the ground to sound their departure, Edie dug a heel in the bay's side to ride it through the gap in the fence. She was so choked with anger she couldn't speak. Once on their land they both turned their horses toward the distant ranch yard as if it had been previously agreed.

"Will you promise to go swimming with me when we get back, momma?" Alison queried in pseudocultured voice. "We have a heated pool." It was a deliberate and acid mockery of Felicia Maddock.

"Didn't you notice? I'm tired. I need my rest," Edie countered bitterly. She caught the glinting light in Alison's eye and unwillingly a laugh was pulled from her throat.

There was no sign of Jerry when they arrived at the ranch. They rubbed their horses down and grained all the stock. As they started toward the house, Jerry drove into the yard in his pickup.

"The next time someone has to go to town, it's going to be me," Alison stated. "It always turns into an all-day affair."

"Did you order the fencing?" Edie ignored her daughter's gibe that Jerry had been loafing all day. They both knew better.

"I ordered it, all right." He fell into step

beside them. The grimness of his expression was echoed in his voice.

"What happened?" She knew there was more to that statement.

"I had to pay cash before they would even order it," he explained.

"What?" Edie stopped, stunned by his announcement.

"Same at the feed store, too, when I stopped to buy grain for the horses."

"Why? Didn't you open an account for us?" Edie demanded.

"I tried," he admitted, "but it seems we don't have any credit established in this area. We either pay on the line or we don't get it. The lumber company did say that if we stayed here a year they would reconsider our application to open an account with them."

"*If* we stayed!" Edie repeated in anger.

"That's what they said." There was a wryly grim twist to his mouth. "The word is out—no credit. It's going to be the same with every supplier."

"And I can guess who put the word out," she muttered under her breath.

"Will Maddock," Alison supplied the name.

"He must have been laughing up his sleeve today." Edie jerked the front door open and stalked into the house.

"Today? Did you see him today?" Jerry held the door for Alison, then followed them both into the house.

"Yes." Alison explained about finding the cattle and running into Maddock and his daughter when they herded them back to Diamond D land. "If his wife is anything like his daughter, she must be a real pain," she concluded.

"She's dead," Jerry informed them.

"How do you know that?" Edie glanced at him in vague surprise.

"I heard somebody mention it—at the feed store, I think. Anyway, I had the impression he lost his wife some time ago." He shrugged.

Edie told herself she wasn't interested in Will Maddock's personal life. It had nothing to do with them. Their problems were more immediate.

"When will the fencing arrive?" she asked to change the subject.

"Part of it will be delivered tomorrow. The rest they are shipping in," Jerry replied.

THE TRUCK WITH THE POSTS AND WIRE came early the next morning. They elected to first replace the fence near the barns so they would have a place to turn the horses loose to graze. It was hard, monotonous labor—pulling out the old, rotten posts, putting in new ones and stringing the barbed wire. Jerry did the phases that called for brute strength, but all three of them were staggering with fatigue at the end of each day.

When the area near the barn was refenced, they turned their efforts to the west property

line where Diamond D cattle were wandering
onto their land. The weather mercifully held,
turning springlike with pleasantly warm after-
noons.

As the sun and work started the perspiration
flowing, Edie removed her jacket and tossed it
inside the cab of the pickup. Alison was farther
up the fence row astride the buckskin gelding,
roping the old fence posts, taking a dally around
the saddle horn to pull them out of the ground
and drag them back to the pickup to be returned
to the house for firewood. She kept ahead of
Jerry, who was setting new posts, and at the
same time chased the curious cattle away from
the fence line, herding any out that wandered in.
It was Edie's task to string the barbed wire and
nail it to the new posts. Dipping a gloved hand
into a sack in the back end of the pickup, she
scraped the bottom to come up with a handful
of metal staples and slipped them into the
pocket of the carpenter's apron around her
waist.

"We're out of staples, Jerry!" she called in a
tired voice.

Shirtless, Jerry's tough, sinewy back muscles
glistened with sweat and dust that turned into
rivulets of mud to streak his skin. He finished
tamping a new post, paused to remove his hat
and wipe his forehead with the back of his arm.
With long, tired strides he started back toward
the truck, stopping to take the shirt he had
draped over the previous fence post.

"I only have a half dozen posts left. I'll go back to the house for another load," he told Edie. "And staples for you. Have Alison help you."

"She's busy," Edie replied after a brief glance that saw her daughter spurring the buckskin toward some young steers racing with tails high through the downed fence line and toward a distant stand of branch-bare cotton-woods. "I'll manage."

With the slamming of the truck door, Edie picked up the trailing strand of the top wire. Even with the protection of leather gloves, she was careful to grip only the wire and avoid the pointed barbs spaced along the wire. Unwinding a long section from the reel, she strung it past one post and onto the second. There she tacked it to the far post and went back to stretch it tight to the first and hammer the staple to wood, holding it in place.

The pickup was bouncing over the uneven ground, disappearing in the direction of the ranch yard, when Edie remembered she had left the wire cutters in the pocket of her jacket. Shrugging, she decided she wouldn't need them before Jerry returned, anyway. With the top wire in place on the next pole, she strung the second and third strands, then went back to the top to repeat the procedure.

Tired and weary, her muscles hadn't quit aching for days. But Edie had learned to block out the discomfort and, robotlike, focus her

concentration on the task. As she tacked the top
wire to a second post, there was a prickling sensation of danger along the back of her neck.
When she turned to walk to the middle post to
stretch the wire taut, she saw Will Maddock sitting astride the big gray buckskin, relaxed in the
saddle and watching her. Edie faltered for a second in mid stride, her pulse leaping in alarm
that she hadn't heard him approach. Aware that
his presence had been noticed, Maddock still
didn't offer a greeting. Pressing her lips
together, Edie decided if he could be rude, so
could she, and she continued to the second post.

"That isn't the way it's done," he criticized
with drawling indifference. "That wire can pull
loose from the far pole and whip right back at
you."

"It's my fence and my problem." Edie
tugged at the top wire to pull it tight. "I can get
along without any supervision from you."

There was a curl in the wire that resisted her
efforts. Edie leaned against the loose section
tacked to the far post to get some leverage. Irritated that she should have any difficulty when
Maddock was watching, she carelessly put too
much strain on the loosely secured section of
wire.

"Look out!" The barked warning came too
late.

Edie heard a pinging snap. Then there wasn't
anything to lean against. She staggered for
balance and heard the whine of recoiling wire.

Sheer instinct raised her hands toward her face as the barbed wire circled her like a whip. A thousand needle-sharp points stabbed into her flesh, piercing her clothes to tear at her skin. She wasn't aware of crying out, but there was the echo of strangled screams in the air.

The wire had tangled at her feet, tripping her up and keeping her from regaining her balance. With each stumbling, staggering step, more flesh was ripped by constricting wire. Her attempts to unwind it only added to the agony. She couldn't even fall to the ground because the wire held her up. It seemed an eternity of time that she was trapped in the web of steel needles, writhing in pain, before a pair of hands held her motionless and gave her support. In actual fact it was only a matter of seconds.

"You stupid, little bitch." A familiar voice was savagely swearing in her face. "You were too damned stubborn to listen. You didn't want my supervision. Maybe you don't want my help, either. Where are your wire cutters? I told you this would happen, but damn fools like you know everything."

The barely controlled fury of his temper whipped at her, slicing into her pride the way the barbs cut her flesh. Yet all the while Maddock was berating her stupidity and stubbornness, he was supporting her with one hand and loosening the strands of wire circling her body. Each breath Edie took was a grunting cry as the straitjacket of wire was not permitting any movement without extracting a penalty of pain. Her eyes were tightly closed, trying to shut out the nightmare.

"Where are the damned wire cutters?" This time Maddock's voice demanded an answer.

"In...the pickup," Edie whispered and cringed in expectation for the barrage of abuse that would follow.

"Of all the—" The explosion stopped as the large hands on her arms tightened. "Don't move," his voice rumbled the order with thunderous warning. "I have some in my saddlebags. Just stand still and don't try to get free. Do you understand? Don't move."

Hysterical laughter started to rise in her throat, because it was so ludicrous to think she could move. "I...can't," she gulped down the bubbling sound.

When he released her, Edie felt a surge of panic. What if he left her? She fought it down as she opened her tear-blurred eyes to watch him eat the distance between her and his horse with long, running strides and return in equal haste with a pair of wire cutters in his hand.

"Have you had a tetanus shot lately?" With his powerful grip he began snipping through the wire strands as if they were pieces of string.

"No...I mean, yes. I have." Tremors of relief were quaking through her as strand after circling strand fell away.

When she was free he gripped her shoulders and lifted her out of the tangle of wire at her feet. Edie swayed unsteadily for a second, but his hands remained to solidly support her. His strength was a silent blessing. Edie tipped her head back to thank him.

"Maddock, I don't—" Before she could express the gratitude she was feeling, he was cutting her off with a hard shake, angry sparks glittering in his flint-gray eyes.

"You stupid, little female!" he raged again in a low growl. "Do you realize how lucky you were?"

"Because you were here? Yes," she nodded. Out of the corner of her eye she saw Alison driving the steers toward the fence.

"No, not because I was here!" Maddock denied that above the noise of the approaching pickup truck. "That barbed wire went around your body. It could just as easily have wrapped itself around your face! It's a miracle you aren't scarred for life. It wouldn't have mattered who the hell was here! Do you understand?"

He shook her again and the blood drained from her face at his explanation. Knowing how easily the barbs had ripped through her clothes and into her skin, Edie closed her eyes at the thought of what might have happened if it had whipped across her unprotected face. Her fingers curled into the sleeves of his black shirt, feeling the iron-hard flesh it covered and gaining strength from him. Distantly she was aware of the slamming of the truck door, but it made no impact on her until she heard Jerry's voice.

"Take your hands off her, Maddock!" he ordered, and grabbed at his arm.

As Maddock loosened his grip to send a fiery glare at her stepson, Alison came running toward her. "Mom, are you all right?" Her eyes widened at the sight of the torn blouse and the blood oozing from the many cuts. She turned on Maddock with a vengeance. "What did you do to her?"

"I didn't do anything to her!" he snapped. "Tenderfeet like you can do it all by yourselves!" With that he was shaking off Jerry's arm as if ridding himself of a pesky fly and striding to his ground-hitched horse.

It was left to Edie to explain, somewhat shakily, all that had happened. While Jerry stayed to put up the fence, Alison drove Edie back to the house to clean the cuts and put some antiseptic on them. Only a few were at all serious, but all of them were painful. Her back, shoulders and arms had suffered the most, but none kept her from working.

The following week it was decided that they had sufficient land fenced and could begin to acquire stock cows to build their herd. Jerry began attending the livestock auctions in the area. It slowed their progress in refencing since Edie and Alison had to work at something else on the days he went to the sale barns.

After three weeks of regular attendance, Jerry didn't have a single cow for his efforts. His story was one of frustration. Every time he made a bid on a pen of cattle, the price went sky-high. Jerry dropped out of the bidding whenever the price exceeded the cattle's market worth.

The day of the next sale it was decided unanimously that all three of them would take a break from their grueling work schedule to attend. It was a grimly silent trio that left their truck and trailer parked with the other ranch vehicles and walked to the sale barn. While Jerry registered and got his number, Edie and Alison went to the snack bar for coffee before the auction started.

The area was a hive of activity. Boisterous male voices hailed one another above the ring of the cash register and orders being given to a harried waitress behind the counter. The smell of cattle and manure permeated the room to make an incongruous mixture with the aroma of freshly baked cinnamon rolls and apple pie. Edie was standing to one side while Alison debated whether she was hungry enough for two rolls instead of just one. For a brief moment Edie considered the fact that neither one of them had to watch their weight, not the way they had been working lately.

"Hey, Cully!" Someone hailed the heavyset man at the cash register. Edie glanced around in idle curiosity. "You're in luck again today. That kid is here. I just saw him registering."

The man took his change and turned to face the stocky cowboy, pushing his way through the crowd of hats and boots and Levi's-clad men. "That kid is slow to catch on, isn't he?" The man gestured to Jerry as Cully grinned and pushed his hat back. "Hasn't he figured out yet that Maddock ain't about to let him buy anything?"

Edie stiffened. To suspect this was what was happening was one thing, but to have it confirmed was quite another. She pretended to be interested in a sign over the counter, but every bit of her attention was centered on the two men, anger making her senses twice as keen.

"Sometimes I wonder how high Maddock would drive the prices," the cowboy was saying. "I wish the kid wouldn't drop out so soon."

"Don't wonder too much," the rancher, Cully, warned. "Hank Farber wondered that last week and started bidding. He wound up owning a pen of expensive stock cattle. Maddock shuts off his bidding the minute the kid does."

"There's no question about it. Maddock wants that ranch."

"Hell! I don't blame him. It sits damned near square in the middle of his place," Cully declared. Alison started to say something to Edie, but she shushed her with a look and sent a glance toward the two men to indicate the reason. "It's got some of the best grassland and hay around here."

"After all Maddock did for Carver, I sure expected that old man to sell the place to him." The cowboy shook his head in absent bewilderment. "Carver never would have hung onto the ranch as long as he did if Maddock hadn't helped him out as much as he did. I know for a fact that Maddock made Carver a standing offer to pay a hundred dollars an acre over the market price. He could have squeezed the old man out of that place a long time ago, but he played fair."

"Maddock is fair, I'll give him that," Cully conceded, and grinned. "Course he can afford to be. That old man, Carver, though, has a streak of cussedness a mile wide. His idea of a practical joke gets a little twisted sometimes. Knowing how much Maddock wanted his ranch, he probably thought it was funny to sell to the widow instead."

"That bothers me. I mean, her being a widow and all." The cowboy frowned and shuffled his feet in discomfort. "I've heard she's quite a looker. She's sunk her money into that ranch, trying to make a home for her and her kids. They sure as hell are working hard trying to fix the place up. I saw them putting in new fence last week, all three of them. Maddock's kinda rough on her."

There was grim satisfaction in knowing someone agreed that they were getting a raw deal. But the rancher Cully was laughing at the statement.

"Hell! Maddock isn't trying to cheat her in the first place," he declared. "He's just trying to force her into selling to him. As for her being a widow, these females have been screaming for equal rights. Now they got them. If they want to play with the boys, they can't expect any special favors. If she can't handle the rough stuff, she'd better go back to the kitchen.''

"Yeah, I guess you're right," the cowboy agreed reluctantly, and looked toward the door. "There's Tom Haven. I've been wanting to see him. See ya, Cully.''

When the two men drifted away, Alison exchanged a look with Edie. "We'd better find Jerry.''

He was in the auction area, halfway up the wooden bleachers that half circled the sale ring. Edie and Alison hurried up the steps to where he was seated and whispered to him what they had overheard, keeping their voices low so others around them couldn't hear.

"There's no point in staying around here, then, is there?" Jerry concluded when they had finished, the line of his mouth thinning out.

"We know the cards are stacked against us, but I think we should play out the hand we've been dealt before we ask for a new deck of cards and change dealers," Edie murmured.

"What do you have in mind?" Jerry eyed her with a glint of admiration and wary amusement.

"I think we should let Maddock go on believing that his dumb tenderfeet haven't caught on to his game plan. Then he won't be expecting us to do anything else," she replied. "We won't talk about it now, though.''

"Okay." He glanced at Alison. "Where's my cup of coffee?"

"Oh, damn." A stricken look of regret widened her eyes. "I left it sitting on the counter. Somebody's probably taken it by now."

"Thanks a lot, sis." He shook his head in resignation and started to rise.

"No, stay here." Edie put a hand on his arm to detain him. "They're bringing the first group of cattle in. I'll get you a cup."

When the cattle were turned into the auction ring it was a signal for everyone loitering in the halls and snack bar to enter at once. Edie had the feeling she was trying to go down an "up" stairway as she edged her way down the steps against the stream of ranchers and cowboys going the opposite way. She was nearly at the bottom when she happened to glance up from the wooden steps straight into a pair of slate-gray eyes. The steps seemed to rock beneath her. The heel of her boot hooked the edge of the board and she would have fallen headfirst down the last step if a familiar pair of hands hadn't caught her and lifted her the last foot to the ground. Edie was conscious of the warm, firm imprint of his hands making themselves felt through the material of her floral blouse. The sensation wasn't unpleasant.

"You'd better watch where you're going," Maddock stated as he released her.

Her gaze flew to his tough, male features, the light of battle sparking in her hazel eyes. "That has a false ring to it, Maddock. Aren't you really hoping that we'll fall flat on our faces?'' she challenged, and didn't wait for him to reply as she pivoted and fought her way against the current of crowd to the snack bar.

CHAPTER FIVE

THE MORNING AFTER THE SALE, Edie leaned against the board fence of the corral and gazed inside at a pair of frisky calves. Several months old, the Hereford calves were already showing the hefty build indicative of their breed. The pair was the only livestock they had succeeded in buying at yesterday's sale. Crossing the corral from haying the horses, Jerry vaulted the fence to stand beside Edie and watch the skittish but curious pair of calves.

"It's up to you, Alison," he said to the tall girl perched atop the rail, "to bring home their mommas from Wyoming."

"I wish you were going instead of me," Alison sighed in apprehension.

"Maddock is convinced that Jerry will be buying our cattle If he goes to Cheyenne, Maddock is going to guess that we're going out-of-state to purchase our stock cows. I don't know how long his influence will continue, but I don't want to find out," Edie replied. "He'll never suspect in a hundred years that we'd send you to buy cattle."

"Neither would I," Alison declared.

"How many horses have you bought at auctions?" Jerry challenged. "You know the procedures. Just make sure you get a health certificate and don't pay more than I told you."

"I don't think I like being an adult," Alison smiled suddenly. "Too much responsibility." She uncurled her long legs to climb down from the rail. "Why do you suppose Maddock let us buy these two calves?"

"Guilty conscience," Edie stated.

"He was probably afraid we might starve, so he let us have a couple of calves that we could butcher in the fall," Alison suggested, and laughed at the thought. "He doesn't know we have an income separate from the ranch."

"Yes—Joe's patents. Maddock probably thinks we are depending on the ranch for our sole support," Edie agreed, her dimples coming into play. "Wouldn't you love to see his face when he finds out differently?"

"I was just thinking," Jerry interrupted their laughter, "I'll bet these calves are a carrot Maddock is dangling in front of our noses to keep us attending the local sales."

"I wouldn't be surprised," Alison agreed.

Edie rested her chin in the cup of her hand to watch the calves nosing a half a bale of hay Jerry had tossed in the corral. She tried to smother a convulsive burst of laughter and only partially succeeded.

"What's so funny?" Jerry eyed her curiously.

"I was just remembering all the grandiose

plans we made last winter." She couldn't keep
the laughter from bubbling in her voice. "We
were going to become big cattle ranchers. And
that's the sum total of our herd!" She waved
toward the two calves. "It would take us longer
to catch and saddle our horses than it would to
round up and brand those calves!"

"I'm afraid you're right," Jerry chuckled.

"We did say we were going to start small,"
Alison reminded them.

"This small?" Edie laughed.

"Why not this small?" Alison challenged,
making a joke out of it. "We can start out with
two the way Noah did. Next year we'll have
four, then eight, then sixteen. Why, in twenty
years we'll have a herd."

Both Edie and Jerry broke out in laughter.
"You have a problem with that theory, Alison." Edie tried to check her laughter long
enough to explain and failed.

Jerry did it for her. "Those are bull calves!"

Then all three were overcome with laughter.
Holding her stomach, Edie leaned heavily
against the fence, tears steaming down her
cheeks. The laughter was a release for all of
them—a release from days of hard work, frustration and tension. It turned something only
mildly amusing into an object of hilarity. Alison
fell against Jerry, laughing too hard to stand on
her own. He circled an arm around her and
reached out to draw Edie inside the curve of his
other arm.

"Edie, you are the only person I know who can find something to laugh about when it looks like your dreams might be dissolving," he declared in a laugh-winded voice.

"Neither one of you would win a prize at being serious," she retorted.

"That's because of you!" Releasing Alison, Jerry circled Edie's waist with his hands and swung her in the air, lifting her above his head. "You are the greatest, Edie!"

"Put me down!" she shrieked in laughter.

Jerry set her on the ground and planted a kiss on her forehead. "I don't care who knows of it," he declared. "Do you, Alison?"

"No." The two exchanged a look that transmitted a silent message.

In the next second Edie was covering her ears as the pair of them tipped their heads back and shouted to the sky at the top of their voices. "Edie Gibbs is the greatest mother in the world!"

"Help, you've stampeded our cattle," Edie laughed as the calves bolted to the far side of the corral.

The helpless laughter was on the verge of starting again until Alison sobered with unexpected swiftness to stare behind them. "Oh, oh," she murmured in a small voice. "We have company."

Edie turned, wiping the tears of laughter from her cheeks. A blue-and-white pickup was parked in the yard, with the driver's door held open by the man standing near it. Maddock shut it when they all looked at him. Edie wondered how a man could be so powerfully built and not look like a muscle-bound freak. He started toward them, and the three of them moved forward together to meet him halfway.

A lazy smile was making attractive grooves in the sun-browned cheeks while his dark gray eyes were silvered with a glint of amusement and curiosity. Edie felt the magnetic pull of his male charm. Sexual and potent, it quivered along her nerve ends.

"I can't remember the last time I saw three people laughing so hard," he remarked. "What was so funny?"

Edie hesitated. "It was a family joke."

"I don't think you would appreciate the humor of it," Alison added.

"Is this a neighborly visit or business?" Edie questioned to change the subject. The indefinable warmth that had been present now vanished as a wintry briskness took over the rancher's manner.

"Business," he admitted.

"We haven't changed our minds about selling," she informed him.

"I didn't think for one minute that you would give up so quickly," Maddock murmured dryly, but his mocking look said they would eventually. "No, it was another matter that I wanted to discuss."

"Which is?" Edie prompted with an icy coolness.

"The below normal rainfall we've had this spring has hurt my grazing land. I don't want to risk overgrazing it, so I'd like to make you an offer to lease your land to run my cattle on," he explained.

"But if we leased our land to you, where would we run our cattle?" she challenged.

"You don't have any cattle, Mrs. Gibbs," he pointed out.

"Not yet," she admitted. "But we hope to acquire a small herd soon. We already have two calves." Let him think they were stupid and gullible, Edie told herself. Anger surged when she saw the glimmer of a smile he tried to conceal.

"I think there would be enough pasture for your *herd* and mine," Maddock replied with mocking inflection.

Playing dumb didn't suit her. "I don't think you want to lease our land because the lack of rainfall has affected yours, Maddock," she said, and was rewarded to see the faint quirk of an eyebrow. "I think your land is overgrazed because it's overstocked. You have been buying a lot of cattle lately." There was a slight narrowing of his gaze. "We aren't interested in leasing you any of our land, but if you want to sell us some of your extra stock cows, we would be glad to discuss that with you. Naturally we would want to pay a fair market value for them, but you are a fair man, aren't you?"

He held her gaze for a long, hard moment. "I'm not interested in selling my cattle at the moment."

"It doesn't look like we can do business, then, does it?" she countered. "Because we aren't interested in leasing you any land."

"Very well." Maddock accepted her answer with a brisk nod. "Let me know if you change your mind."

"Yes," Edie agreed with a honeyed smile. "And you let us know if you change yours."

"Of course." The slanting line of his mouth formed a smile of grudging approval with a hint of admiration. Edie had a fleeting glimpse of it before he turned to walk back to his truck. Maddock had let her claim victory in this battle, but the war wasn't over. The war of the sexes was never over. A tingling shock ran down Edie's spine. Where had she got the idea that this was a man-woman struggle? That was absurd. It was the ranch they were fighting over. Maddock wanted it, and she was just as determined not to let him have it. It had nothing to do with sex.

Inadvertently she recalled the firm grip of his hands when he had caught her yesterday to save her from falling down the auction steps. And the previous time when he'd held her, supported her while he swiftly and expertly dispensed with the ribbon of barbed wire. Unbidden, she remembered the warm, musky smell of leather, sweat and horse mixed with the scent of shaving lotion. The combination was unique to Maddock, a stamp of his male individuality.

Even now the virile scent of him lingered in her memory, honing her senses to a keen edge. Just for a second, Edie permitted a spark of curiosity to wonder what kind of lover he would be—masterful, knowing; both of those without a doubt. Like her, Maddock had been married, so making love would hold no secrets. But his hands, when they explored her body, would they...

Heat flamed molten hot over her flesh when Edie realized what she was visualizing in her mind. What was the matter with her? She had never indulged in such fantasies about Joe before she married him. Edie rationalized that away with the reasoning that she had been innocent of the act itself, and she hadn't been tempted to use her imagination. Edie was shocked that Maddock had aroused her sexual curiosity when not a single other man had—not even Joe, the one person who might have.

"Why the frown, mom?" Alison's question was light and innocent, yet it pulled Edie sharply out of her reverie.

Maddock's truck had completed its circle and was bouncing over the rutted land away from the ranch yard. Edie was struck again by the abrupt way he kept entering and exiting her life.

"Just once I'd like to hear that man say hello and goodbye," she retorted.

"It would be a novelty," Jerry agreed.

"Well?" He glanced at the two of them with a raised eyebrow. "Shall we get to work?"

"Yes." There was a grimness in Edie's agreement. "We have a lot to do, and I want Alison to leave first thing in the morning."

A VIOLENT SPRING THUNDERSTORM ARRIVED on the heels of Alison's departure. The deluge confined Edie to the house, where there was plenty of work to be done. Jerry used the time to work on the tractor, which had been running roughly, and make certain the hay baler would be ready when they needed it.

Intermittent rain showers plagued the area for three days. The only ray of brightness came from Alison's telephone call of a successfully accomplished mission and the date when the shipment of stock cattle would arrive.

The rain made preparation for the impending shipment impossible. Edie kept herself busy with the house, which had been neglected recently, but she would have preferred to be outside. All day long she consoled herself with the knowledge that the rain was needed. Proof of that was demonstrated by the way the parched ground soaked it up as quickly as it fell.

Yet at night when she was alone in the front bedroom with the fingers of rain drumming on the roof, Edie tossed restlessly in the double bed. She finally tossed the pillow next to hers onto the floor, but it hadn't helped to ease her tension. Most of her married life she had gone to bed alone while Joe had puttered in his workshop, so why did sleeping alone bother her now?

She tried to convince herself that these yearnings tormenting her were natural. After all, hadn't she read that a woman's libido reached its peak in the mid thirties? Grief had no doubt suppressed these longings. Now that it had begun to wane, it was natural they would surface.

And there was a logical reason why the image of Will Maddock's face kept flitting through her mind. With the cattle on their way, she was subconsciously trying to imagine his reaction to the news. That's why she kept seeing those smoke-gray eyes look at her with such unnerving steadiness, those hard-cast features etched with strong, sun-creased lines and that mouth cut in a male shape. These recollections had nothing to do with the brief flight of fancy her senses had taken the last time she'd seen him.

Stifling a moan with her fist, Edie rolled onto her side and faced the empty width of the bed. Her hand reached out to the emptiness beside her. "I did love you, Joe," she whispered tightly. A little voice inside reminded her that there were many kinds of love, and the force of one did not negate the strength of another. Many kinds of love existed side by side, one not diminishing another. She hugged the blankets more tightly around her and closed her eyes, listening to the drumming message of the spring rain on the roof.

The sun came out the morning the semitrailertrucks arrived with the cattle. With Alison back and teaming up with Jerry, it was easy for Edie to forget her restive stirrings and join in with their jubilant spirits. Herding the cattle to a section of the range where there was plenty of grass and water was a festive occasion.

It was after one o'clock when they reached the valley meadow. Within minutes the cattle were scattering out to graze in the knee-deep grass, lush and green after the rain. Everything was washed clean, the air crystal clear, the colors of the trees and hills more brilliant than before. Wild flowers were bobbing their heads in the tall grasses and peeking out of rocky crags.

"Let's eat our lunch on the saddle of that ridge." Alison motioned toward the hollowed crest between two hills, treeless and possessing an unobstructed view of the valley.

Her suggestion was quickly seconded by Jerry, and the three of them rode their horses halfway up the slope and tied them in the shade of a stand of white-barked aspens. Rocky boulders offered hard seats for them to sit on while they ate their sandwiches and sipped at hot coffee from the thermos. Yet the plainness of the food didn't alter the picnic atmosphere that predominated.

"I really feel as if we own a ranch now," Alison murmured.

Looking down at the valley floor where the mixed herd of Hereford and Angus grazed, Edie studied the shiny black hides that glistened in the sunlight and contrasted with the rust-red coats of the white-faced Herefords. She, too, had the feeling that what had long been a dream had finally taken the form of reality.

"We've worked hard these last months," Jerry added in an equally quiet voice. "But looking down there at that sight is quite a reward in itself."

There was a clatter of hooves on stone behind them. Edie turned to see a horse and rider top the crest and rein in. Unconsciously she rose to meet the silent challenge of Will Maddock's presence, a little pulse hammering in her throat.

"One of his spies must have told him about the cattle, and he had to see it for himself to believe it," Alison whispered in a caustic under-breath.

Except for a cursory glance at the herd grazing in the valley, Maddock exhibited no further interest in the cattle. His attention seemed to be focused on Edie. To enforce the impression, he guided his horse over the exposed rock face to where she was standing. He rested his gloved hands on the saddle horn as he tipped his head down to look at her.

"The storm knocked down a tree on your fence line. I thought you should know," he stated. "It's wise to check for damage after hard storms. Sometimes a small creek can turn into a raging torrent that wipes out a whole section of fence. Flash floods aren't uncommon here." -

The sting of his criticism smarted. Edie was well aware that he was taking the opportunity to point out how inexperienced they were. A trio of tenderfeet, he'd called them.

"It was thoughtful of you to come all this way to tell us." But there was a bite to her polite response.

"I don't know if my reason could be described as thoughtful, Mrs. Gibbs." On that cryptic note he turned his head to sweep an experienced eye over the herd of cattle below them. "That's a fine-looking bunch. They're carrying Wyoming brands, aren't they?"

"Yes," Edie admitted, and realized he could possibly tell her the name and location of the ranch that the brands were registered to.

The buckskin stamped a foot at a buzzing fly, and the saddle leather creaked under its rider's weight. "You must have made a quick trip to Wyoming and back." Maddock addressed the remark to Jerry, who was leaning a hip against the boulder near Edie.

"I didn't go." Jerry calmly met the gray gaze leveled at him. "Alison bought the herd."

"Yes," she piped up a little smugly, and strolled over to stand near her brother. "It was amazing how much cheaper the cattle sold for there than the price they were bringing here at the local sale barns. Even with the shipping costs added in we saved money."

"So now you're in the cattle business." It was a flat statement that ventured no opinion.

"And we're going to be successful at it," Alison declared rashly. "You shouldn't underestimate the Gibbs family, Mr. Maddock."

There was a suggestion of a smile around his firm mouth. The glint in his eyes was unmistakable as his glance encompassed all three of them, lingering for a fraction of a second on Edie. "You can be sure I won't." Applying pressure on the bridle bit, he signaled the buckskin to back up, then pivoted the horse at a right angle to send it up the crest.

CHAPTER SIX

"You're right, mother," Alison muttered in an irritated breath. "It would be a novelty if he ever said goodbye."

Edie dragged her gaze from the crest of the saddle-back ridge where Maddock had disappeared. She had just begun to enjoy a feeling of peace and contentment before he showed up. Now she felt disjointed, at odds within herself.

"It doesn't really matter what he didn't say," Jerry said, straightening from the boulder. "He did give us some sound advice. We should check to see what damage the storm did. We might as well split up and cover more ground."

"I suppose," Alison sighed, and Edie let her agreement be a silent one as they walked down the slope to the trees where they had tied their horses.

After mounting up, they fanned out to take three different directions. Edie hadn't chosen the section of boundary fence she was to check; the choice had been made for her when Jerry and Alison had chosen the other two. At the time there hadn't been any reason to object until she saw the rider walking his horse and thought of an excellent reason—Will Maddock.

Her gloved hand tightened automatically on the reins of the bay gelding. It pulled up abruptly out of its trot into a prancing halt. She glanced anxiously around her, but both Alison and Jerry were already out of sight. What was more, Maddock had already seen her.

Edie was angry that it hadn't occurred to her this was the logical route Maddock would take back to his ranch. Or had it? Had her subconscious buried the knowledge? It was too late for such thoughts to be occurring to her.

Her objective was to check the fences in this region. She had a choice of either following Maddock at a distance or riding on at a normal pace as if it didn't matter. It didn't matter, she argued silently. She wasn't afraid of him.

Digging in her heels, she sent the bay horse forward at an easy lope. Maddock didn't exactly wait for her, but she caught up with him easily. The ground became rough beneath her horse. Edie had to let the bay choose its own pace or risk laming it, which meant she had to ride alongside Maddock.

"I see you decided to take my advice," he commented.

"About checking the storm damage, yes," she agreed stiffly, not turning her gaze from the front, but conscious of his gray eyes sliding over her. "About selling the ranch to you, no."

"I don't recall advising you to sell to me," Maddock replied dryly.

"That's true," Edie recalled with a touch of disdain that was alien to her nature. "I believe you said we would break under the pressure."

"You will eventually." He reached into his shirt pocket for a cigarette and, one-handed, cupped a lighted match to the tip.

"You are wrong, Maddock." Edie tried to keep her gaze from straying to his craggy profile and the way his eyes squinted against the smoke curling from the cigarette in his mouth. He was too rawly masculine. "I think we have proved we don't break under pressure...even your pressure."

"My pressure?" His mouth curved without smiling.

"Admit it, Maddock," Edie insisted a shade triumphantly. "You are upset because we outsmarted you and bought our cattle elsewhere after you tried to keep us from buying any cattle here. You are irritated because you were bested by a bunch of greenhorns."

"No, I'm not irritated," he countered smoothly. "And I don't deny that I kept you from making any successful bids on cattle. You can call that pressure if you like."

"What else do you call it?" she retorted. When he didn't answer she demanded, "Did you really think it would work?"

"If you had been a bunch of faint-hearted, dumb tenderfeet, yes, it would have worked,

because you would have given up in another
month and sold out. You showed you were stubborn and intelligent. But it doesn't change the
eventual outcome.''

"That's where you're wrong, Maddock.''
Edie was angry that he was so damned sure of
himself. "We aren't selling. And if the day ever
comes when we do, I'd sell it to the devil before
I'd sell it to you.''

"And you are making a mistake.'' He blew
out a stream of smoke and gave her a long, hard
look, his hands resting on the saddle horn while
his body moved with the rocking motion of the
walking horse.

"I'm not making any mistake,'' she denied,
unable to withstand the force of that dark gray
gaze.

"Yes, you are. You're taking this personally.
I have nothing against you or your family. If
you want to play cowboy, go somewhere else. I
want the ranch. It's that simple. You have it. I
want it and I'm going to do everything I can to
persuade you to sell—to me.''

"Persuade? Force, you mean,'' Edie corrected tightly. "Doesn't it matter to you that
this ranch is our home?''

"It isn't your home,'' he denied without
hesitation or emotion. "Wherever it is you're
from in Illinois, that's your home.''

"That *was* our home. *This* is our home now.''
Strangely, that was true. This was where she felt
she belonged now. Their home and life in Illinois seemed a lifetime ago.

"Don't sink your roots too deep," he warned.

The boundary fence was ahead of them. Blocking their way was a tall pine tree, toppled by the storm. Its trunk was charred where lightning had struck it. The top third of it was resting atop the fence. A post taking most of its weight had kept the newly strung barbed wire from snapping.

Ignoring Maddock, Edie reined her horse toward the tree and stopped near the fence. Since she had expected Maddock to ride on, she dismounted to untie the lariat hanging from her saddle. She glanced over the suede-covered seat of her saddle to see Maddock swinging off his horse.

"What are you doing?" she questioned.

"I'm giving you a hand." He untied his coiled rope and walked toward the tree.

Hurrying, Edie reached it ahead of him and began tying the end of her rope around the tapered trunk. "I don't happen to need your help."

"I'm sure you can manage on your own." He expertly tied his knot while she was still fumbling with hers. "The same way you did with the barbed wire."

She flashed him an angry look and jerked the knot tight. Walking back to her horse, she stepped into the saddle and looped the other end of the rope around the saddle horn. Maddock was already astride his buckskin, the rope dallied around his horn and waiting for her.

Reining the bay at an angle away from the tree, she walked it forward until the rope was stretched taut across her thigh. Out of the corner of her eye, Edie was aware that Maddock had set his horse at a parallel line with hers.

The bay felt the weight at the end of the rope, the resistance, and fidgeted nervously. Patting its neck, she urged it forward and looked back. Pine branches were making rustling noises against the fence. Slowly the top half of the tree was beginning to move. There was the splintering crack of wood as the tree trunk began to split from the lightning-struck stump. Then it snapped and the tree slithered off the fence and crashed to the ground, limbs cracking and breaking, the taut wire singing.

The rope went slack and Edie immediately halted her horse, its dark head tossing nervously. She ignored the fact that Maddock was already on the ground walking to untie his rope from the tree when she dismounted. A white-hot tension was racing through her as she followed him.

Pulling the tree off the fence had tightened the knot. Edie had to work to get it loose. By the time she had it untied, Maddock already had his rope recoiled. His swiftness and adeptness made her feel clumsy and slow in comparison.

"I didn't ask you to help me, so don't expect any thanks." She jerked the rope free and began coiling it into a circle.

"I didn't expect any thanks. I didn't get any

when I cut you out of that wire or when I saved you from falling down the steps. If neither of those warranted an expression of gratitude, this certainly doesn't.'' His indifferent glance was cool and gray. "Your manners leave something to be desired.''

"My manners!'' If Edie had felt a twinge of guilt, his last statement chased it away. "You don't even have the common courtesy to say anything as polite as hello or goodbye. You're too busy throwing your weight around! I imagine you've been pushing people around for quite a while. It's high time somebody started shoving back.''

"You?'' Mocking laughter glinted in his look although there was no change in his expression.

There had been too much tension, too many seething emotions held in check for too long. The thread of control holding them had worn thin. At his taunt it snapped. Edie struck out at the male features that had tormented her in so many ways. The leather of her glove absorbed much of the stinging contact with his cheek, protecting her palm.

Her arm had barely finished its arc when it was seized in a viselike grip. With a rough yank Maddock hauled her against his chest. His retaliation was too swift and caught Edie unprepared to resist. Her head was thrown back and her wide hazel eyes were drawn to his face. The white mark on his cheek where she had hit him was turning red. There was a thunderous shade to his gray eyes, a violent Dakota storm about to break over her head.

An instinct for survival made her struggle. With her free hand Edie pushed at his chest and strained against the iron band that circled her waist. It didn't seem to matter how much she turned and twisted, she couldn't elude the contact with his powerfully muscled build.

"Let me go!" she demanded angrily, and tried to jerk her wrist free of his grip, but he used the downward movement to fold her arm behind her back and force her more fully to his length.

"You did this deliberately, didn't you?" Maddock accused grimly.

"I'm not sorry I slapped you," Edie flashed. "I'm only sorry I didn't hit you harder."

He continued as if he hadn't even heard her, anger blazing in his eyes. "You deliberately provoked this so you could make me aware that beneath these boy's clothes there is a woman's body."

"No!" she gasped the stunned denial.

She stopped struggling, suddenly conscious that the writhings of her body were a provocation in themselves. She was no match for his strength. While he had easily checked her attempts to wrestle out of his hold, his hands had succeeded in fitting her intimately to the contours of his frame. Her hips were pressed firmly to the solid columns of his thighs and the thrusting angle of his hips. While trying to ease the pressure on the arm he'd twisted behind her back, she had arched the roundness of her breasts fully against his chest.

"How long has your husband been dead?" Maddock demanded. "Has abstinence built up your sexual frustration until you can't stand it?"

A strangled cry of protest and denial was ripped unintelligibly from her throat. His accusation was too close to the wayward thoughts that had been running through her mind these past days. That knowledge flamed through her body. She had to escape him before his nearness caused a purely physical response. In a last bid for her freedom, Edie kicked at his shin with the pointed toe of her boot and scored a direct hit. He cursed in pain under his breath and relaxed his grip just enough for Edie to twist free. She tried to run, but he grabbed at her arm.

"Oh, no, you don't!" His fingers closed on her sleeve, catching just enough material to half turn her around.

Her foot became tangled in the coiled rope she'd dropped. Edie lost her balance and tumbled backward. She was conscious of her legs becoming tangled with his as she fell, toppling him with her. The impact with the ground momentarily knocked the wind out of her.

CHAPTER SEVEN

"YOU LITTLE HELLCAT!" Before Edie could recover her breath, Maddock rolled on top of her, captured the hands that would have pushed him away and pinned them to the ground above her head.

Crushed by his weight, Edie couldn't move. Helpless in the face of his brute strength, she was conscious that the fall had knocked her hat off, spilling the chestnut length of her hair over the ground. But she was more conscious of the pressing heat of his body and the way it heightened the earthy smell of him. She tried not to breathe and inhale his stimulating scent.

But there wasn't any way she could block out the feel of him, all that solidly muscled weight flattening her curves. It was too suggestive lying beneath him this way. Edie was afraid to move in case Maddock discovered it, too. Her gaze became centered on the open collar of his shirt. She didn't dare look any higher, aware of the tanned column of his throat and the hard, male features so close to her own. She could feel the warmth of his breath against her face, a sensual caress that she tried desperately to ignore.

There was a moment of stillness when neither moved. It stretched endlessly until some powerful, invisible force compelled Edie to lift her gaze. It traveled slowly up the corded muscles of his neck, dwelling for an instant on the pulse she saw hammering in his throat. In the space of another second her eyes became fascinated by the strong male outline of his mouth. Finally she met the magnetic darkness of his gaze.

"Maddock—" It was a plea, whether to be released or to be kissed, she never had a chance to find out for herself.

"Shut up, Edie." The husky order was issued as his mouth lowered onto hers.

The shape of her lips was explored with consummate ease, every curve and contour investigated with sensual thoroughness. Her mouth became soft and pliant under the influence of his kiss. Edie couldn't stop the quivering response that trembled through her. There was a physical hunger that refused to be suppressed any longer.

When the sweet demand of his mouth seduced her lips apart, a languorous warmth invaded her limbs until they seemed to melt to his shape. A fever was born, contagious and hot. Her arms were released and allowed to find their way around the breadth of his shoulders. His arms forced their way beneath her and tried to absorb her into his flesh.

A blackness threatened to claim her. Turning her head, she eluded his mouth and gasped for a breath. "You're hurting me, Maddock," she murmured, because she doubted that he knew his own strength.

He levered himself above her, completely removing his weight. "Am I too heavy for you?" His husky voice was an evocative caress in itself.

Her lashes fluttered open as her gaze sought the face inches away from hers. She became fascinated by the sun-creased lines fanning out from the corners of his eyes and the slashing grooves that framed his mouth. She wanted to trace their paths as if they would provide the answer to the mystery of this man who could incite her to such anger. . . and such passion.

Edie could breathe again, but she didn't know if she wanted to. There was still his question to answer, and Maddock was waiting for it. "Yes. . . I mean, no." She saw the satisfaction glittering in his dark gray eyes as he watched confusion and desire chasing each other across her expression. "Oh, Maddock, I don't know," she admitted finally with a feeling that she had admitted a lot more than that.

"I never thought you'd be at a loss for a quick, decisive reply. This is an occasion," he murmured complacently and shifted his position to lie along her side with only a fraction of his weight resting on her.

His mouth moved to reclaim possession of her lips, consuming them with a lazy hunger that fed her desire. She felt the smoothness of a leather-gloved hand cup the side of her head, a thumb sliding down her neck to the base of her throat. Then the caressing hand was abruptly removed, and Edie was vaguely aware of some movement above her head. When the hand returned it was minus the glove. The sensitive skin of her neck delighted in the pleasing roughness of his callused touch, responding to it the way her lips responded to the masterful seduction of his kiss.

Once his hand and fingers had explored every inch of her neck, his mouth followed them up to claim the territory as his personal property. His tongue seared his brand in all the sensitized hollows while his hand continued its discovery trail, pushing the collar of her blouse aside to investigate her collarbone and the point of her shoulder. Quivers of sheer passion trembled through her bones. Somewhere in the back of her mind a sweet turmoil was going on, but she was too conscious of the havoc his mouth was creating at a point below her collarbone. When he paused and lifted his head to let his fingers trace the area his lips had just claimed, she had to swallow a moan of protest.

"Is this mark from the barbed wire?" Maddock questioned in a low, taut voice that vibrated through her.

Edie moved a hand as if to touch the place, but the small scar was undoubtedly the result of that misadventure. "I...yes." What did it matter now? In her love-disturbed state she was interested only in this incident.

Maddock pressed a kiss to the mark as if to speed the healing process and eliminate the blemish from her silken skin. "I'll never forget that day and the sight of you trussed up like a little brown hen in that wire," he murmured against her neck as he slowly worked his way up to her lips. "After I cut you free, my first reaction was to wring your pretty little neck for getting yourself into such a predicament. So I did the next best thing by shaking you. But my second reaction—" he spoke against her lips, tantalizing their outline with the promise of a kiss while their breaths combined "—would have made the cockiest rooster proud. If your protectors hadn't arrived we would have been making love then instead of waiting until now."

A tiny animal sound of pleasure came from her throat under the driving possession of his kiss. Phrases of his sentences began spinning in her mind. His hand had found its way inside her blouse and his fingers slid inside the cup of her brassiere to encircle her breast.

No other man had made love to her except Joe. Maddock would be the first, and the experience promised to be like nothing she'd ever known before. But wasn't it supposed to mean something? Did it? It was all happening too fast. Edie realized she wasn't ready for this—whatever it was.

With a muffled groan she twisted and rolled

away from him fighting the traitorous waves of regret. As she scrambled to her feet, common sense insisted that her decision was wise. What did she know about Maddock? What did she think of him? Was it loneliness that had made her respond, or something else?

"Edie?" His voice was low and questioning, puzzled yet insistent that she explain.

She realized he was standing very close to her. The knowledge had a somersaulting effect on her heart, and Edie took a deep breath to calm her panicking nerves. The action drew her attention to the unbuttoned front of her blouse. She quickly tried to fasten the buttons, but it was a fumbling attempt. She damned the gloves that turned her fingers into thumbs.

A hand touched her shoulder, and she jerked away from the searing contact. "No." It was both a denial and a rejection. The next time he touched her, there was nothing gentle in the contact as Maddock forcibly turned her around to face him. Edie drew back as far as his hand would allow and refused to meet the cold steel of his probing gaze. "Let me go, Maddock," she requested stiffly. "I am not in the mood—" The rest of the sentence was lost in a gasp of pain when his fingers tightened to dig into her flesh. She was about to say she wasn't in the mood to argue, but Maddock interpreted the words as they stood.

"Not in the mood," he repeated in tight-lipped anger. He clamped a large hand on her

hip and yanked her toward him, molding the
lower half of her body to his length and impressing on her flesh how very potently he was
in the mood. "What am I supposed to do?
Silently accept the fact that I'm to be sexually
frustrated because a lonely widow has got an
attack of cold feet? You let me become this
aroused, Edie."

"I know it." She suppressed a shudder of
longing. Her aching dissatisfaction wasn't
helped by the knowledge of his need. She hadn't
intentionally led him on, even if that was the
way it seemed. "Let me go."

For an instant Edie thought Maddock was going to ignore her brittle request. Then she was
released and standing free, the subject of the ac-
cusing rake of his gaze.

"I didn't do anything you didn't want me to
do," Maddock stated.

Unable to meet his eyes, she reached down to
pick up the half-coiled rope near her feet. She
concentrated on coiling the rest of it while she
answered him. "All right. I admit that I wanted
to be kissed and fondled, but I'm not so
desperate that I wanted to have sex with you."
She feared that she had responded to him out of
a need to be loved as only a man can love a
woman.

Her gaze ricocheted off his narrowed look.
Turning, she walked to her horse and tied the
lariat to the saddle. Raw nerves screamed at the
way his eyes followed her every move.

"How long had you been married before your husband died?" Maddock questioned.

"Eighteen years." She stepped into the stirrup and swung into the saddle. Feeling secure now that she was mounted, Edie glanced at him. "Why?"

He had gathered the reins to his horse and mounted in one fluid movement. "I was just wondering who wore the pants in your marriage—you or your husband?" There was something taunting in his steady regard as he squared his horse around to face hers.

"Joe did, of course," she retorted.

"Of course?" A thick brow arched at the phrase. The saddle creaked as Maddock shifted his weight deeper into the seat. "I wonder why I have the feeling you told him which pair to put on."

Resentment burned hot through her veins. She had made a lot of the decisions, but she had always consulted Joe. His implication that she had been the boss irritated Edie. She refused to admit it was because it carried a grain of truth.

"I'm certain that you wish I was a helpless female incapable of standing up to you. You would have had my ranch by now, wouldn't you, Maddock?" Edie challenged.

He nudged his horse forward until his leg was rubbing against hers. "Instead of wearing a man's clothes, Edie, you should try filling a man's bed." The line of his mouth curved but it didn't smile.

"Yours, I suppose!" she flashed angrily, and slapped the reins to her horse's rump to send it lunging into a canter that swiftly carried her away from Maddock toward the ranch house.

Edie didn't slow her horse to a walk until she was out of sight. She choked on a sob and forced it down. Her pride and self-respect were soothed by the knowledge that although she had been vulnerable to his attraction for a little while, she had overcome it. No doubt Maddock would be pleased if she was plagued by that brief interlude. It would be one more weapon he could use against her. Well, she wasn't going to let it happen. It hadn't meant anything except that she was human and capable of being made to respond. She certainly wasn't going to hide from Maddock in the future because of it. After all, he was just a man.

THREE DAYS LATER Edie was with Jerry and Alison on the south boundary putting in the new fence. The other three sides to their ranch had been refenced. When this was in, they could begin on the inner pastures, which wouldn't be for a couple of days yet.

At the sound of a horse and rider approaching, Edie mentally braced herself to meet Maddock. But when she looked up, it was his daughter who was reining in her horse. And she was alone.

"Have you seen my father?" Even as she made the imperious demand of Edie, her gaze was straying with cool, feminine interest to Jerry, who was shirtless. His tanned muscles bulged as he drove a fence post into the ground.

"No," Edie replied, barely pausing in her work. "And I'm not expecting to." Just in case there was some question.

"He said something about moving some cattle. I just thought he might have been by here." Felicia shrugged as if it didn't matter.

"I haven't seen him," Edie repeated, injecting supreme indifference into her voice.

"Who is he? Your hired hand?" The haughty question was spoken in a voice deliberately loud enough for Jerry to hear.

"No." With a sidelong glance at Jerry, Edie saw he had paused to look up, so she made the introduction. "This is my stepson, Jerry Gibbs. Jerry, meet Felicia Maddock."

The vibrantly attractive brunette walked her flashy chestnut over to where Jerry was working. An overabundance of pride made her smile appear aloof, but there was no mistaking the avid interest in her blue eyes.

"Hello, Felicia." Jerry's wide smile was natural, his voice was a little winded from his physical exertion.

"It looks like you're working hard," the girl observed, and hooked a knee around the saddle horn, leaning a hand on the cantle. The provocative pose was reminiscent of the kind from the western calendars.

Jerry's gaze flicked over her in mild amusement and a little interest. "It's the only way the work gets done." He began tamping the post into the ground.

"Daddy is certainly going to appreciate all the improvements you've made on this place," Felicia remarked in an attempt at adult cynicism. "It will be just that much less he'll have to do when he buys it."

"Presuming, of course, that we sell it," Jerry reminded her, mocking her with his smile.

"You will," she replied with false confidence. "You can ask anybody. A Maddock always gets what he wants."

"Is that right?" Jerry continued with his work.

"You don't mind if I watch you, do you?" Felicia questioned.

"No, I don't mind." With that post in place, Jerry picked up his tools and moved on to set the next one. Felicia slid her boot back in the stirrup and reined her horse after him.

Alison pulled the barbed wire tight while Edie hammered a staple into the wood post to hold it. "I wonder if Jerry feels properly honored that Felicia is flirting with him," Alison murmured in dry sarcasm.

Edie glanced in Jerry's direction. The brunette was leaning on her saddle horn toward him, talking about something, but at this distance she couldn't hear what the girl was saying.

"She is an attractive girl," Edie said, although she silently agreed that Felicia was out to make a conquest.

"The trouble is she knows it," Alison muttered.

Felicia Maddock stayed for about an hour. Not one sentence was directed at anyone else except Jerry. As far as she was concerned, Alison and Edie didn't exist. Although Felicia did the bulk of the talking, Jerry did respond at the appropriate times, but he didn't slacken his pace.

As she turned her horse to ride away, she tossed a mocking, "Don't work too hard, Jerry," over her shoulder.

"Don't work too hard, Jerry," Alison mimicked. "You'd better be careful, brother of mine. She wants to wrap you around her little finger."

"Oh, yeah?" He paused to wipe the sweat from his neck, and laughter twinkled in his eyes. "She's just a kid."

"She's eighteen if she's a day," Alison retorted. "And I wouldn't like to see her get her claws into you."

"I think Jerry can take care of himself," Edie inserted.

"Thanks, Edie," Jerry smiled. "To hear Alison talk, you'd think it was months since I'd seen a girl." Then with an impish wink he added, "Which it has been."

"You just watch that girl," Alison warned.

"I will," he promised with a roguish grin.

Jerry had ample opportunity in the three days

it took them to finish the fencing, because Felicia Maddock "happened" to ride by every day. Each time she stayed about an hour, talking and flirting with Jerry, who neither encouraged her nor discouraged her.

Having the girl there automatically turned Edie's thoughts to Maddock. She studied Felicia, noting the similarities of their features and wondering if the differences came from Felicia's mother. This thought prompted a curiosity about Maddock's late wife and, ultimately, the question of why he hadn't remarried. With his virile tough looks and status, there wouldn't be a lack of candidates eager to fill the position. But Edie didn't ask a single question because she didn't want to admit an interest in him, not even a casual one—partly because the feelings he aroused in her could be described as anything but casual.

Saturday was the day reserved for their weekly trip into town for supplies. The advent of June had also brought the annual influx of summer tourists to the area. The streets of Custer were crowded with vehicles and pedestrians. It took almost twenty minutes to find a place to park. Then it was several blocks away from the main business district.

"From now on we'd better come to town in the middle of the week," Edie suggested.

"You won't get any argument from me." Jerry locked the door of the pickup before stepping up the curb to the sidewalk. "Do you want to meet me at the hardware store in an hour?''

"We should be through with our shopping and errands by then," Edie agreed after a questioning glance at her daughter.

"Most of them, anyway," Alison nodded.

With the crowd of tourists filling the sidewalks and the buildings of the colorful western-storefronted town, it took longer than they anticipated. The hour had passed, yet Edie had acquired only half the items on her list.

"We'd better meet Jerry and catch the rest of the things later, mom," Alison advised when they finally made it through the long line at a cash register. "At this rate it's going to take us all day instead of all morning."

Jostled by a customer who was attempting to exit the store at the same time Edie was going out the door, she wasn't able to immediately reply. "You're right," she sighed with a trace of disgust, "on both counts."

They crossed the street to the hardware store and went inside, but they couldn't find Jerry. None of the clerks recalled seeing him, but the store was crowded. It was possible he had been in and already gone. They went back outside.

"What do you think we should do?" The corners of Alison's mouth were pulled grimly down by her fading patience. "Should we wait here in case he's late, too? Or walk all the way back to where the truck is parked to see if he's there?"

"With all these people, we could pass him on the street and never notice him." Edie frowned at the hopelessness of trying to recognize a person in this sea of faces streaming by.

"There he is!" Alison pointed across the street. An eyebrow arched coolly. "And will you look at who has waylaid him? Miss High-and-mighty herself," she declared at the same moment that Edie recognized Felicia Maddock was the one who had stopped Jerry to talk to him. "I heard him mention to her yesterday that we'd be in town today."

"Alison, you make it sound as if she arranged to meet him," Edie chided.

"I wouldn't put it past her," was the shrugging answer.

Edie noticed the proprietorial way Felicia held onto Jerry's forearm. And she also noticed the smiling way Jerry observed the action, amused, indulgent and not exactly indifferent. For a brief moment she wondered if the Gibbs family was naturally susceptible to the Maddock brand of charm. With a wide beguiling smile, Felicia said something to Jerry. His reply must not have been what the brunette expected to hear, because she abruptly withdrew her hand from his arm, her expression freezing in an attempt to hide hurt anger.

"It looks like Miss Prissy Pants had her fur ruffled," Alison murmured with undisguised glee.

Edie flashed her daughter a reproving look, but Alison was watching her brother cross the street to the hardware store. When he reached

the other side where they waited, his gaze ran
over them in apology.

"Sorry I'm late. I hope you haven't been
waiting long," he said.

"Long enough to see you with Felicia," Alison
murmured archly.

He glanced across the street in the direction
that Felicia had taken. There was a wistful glint
in his eyes that Edie noticed. "Yeah, I talked to
her for a few minutes," he admitted without
comment.

"What did you say that upset her?" Alison
wanted to know.

"She asked me to buy her a cup of coffee, and
I—" Jerry paused, a vague frown clouding his
expression.

"And what?" Alison prompted.

A wry smile twisted his mouth. "I told her that
if I wanted to buy her a cup of coffee I would do
the asking."

"No wonder she reacted as if you had slapped
her," Alison murmured.

"But you wanted to ask her?" Edie suggested.

"Let's just say I might have if she wasn't—"
He hesitated over the reason.

Edie supplied what she believed was the obvious one. "Maddock's daughter."

"I could have overlooked that," Jerry corrected. "What I was going to say is if she wasn't
such a spoiled brat." Adeptly he changed the
subject. "I hope you haven't finished all your
shopping."

"Hardly." Alison rolled her eyes expressively.

"If you don't need her, Edie, I could use Alison's help. I brought a couple of gates and a metal water trough. The lumberyard is so busy that they don't have anybody who can help me load them," Jerry explained.

"Sure, I'll help," Alison volunteered.

"I think I can manage without her," Edie agreed dryly.

"We'll meet you somewhere for lunch. That café by the corner?" he suggested.

"Okay. At one-thirty after the lunch hour rush is over," Edie suggested.

CHAPTER EIGHT

THERE WAS STILL TIME before Edie had to meet Alison and Jerry, so she wandered along the sidewalk beneath the shade of the overhang. A dress in a store window caught her eye, and she stopped to admire it. Made from a soft, melon-colored fabric, its design was cunningly simple, revealing a lot of skin and shoulder while avoiding the plunging look.

Its obvious femininity made a mockery of the image reflected by the plate-glass window. A slender, dark-haired woman looked back at Edie, her shapely figure covered in an uninspired combination of slacks and a knit top, a unisex, uniage outfit. Her gaze strayed back to the dress that needed the roundness of a woman's body to properly show off both.

"Hi, mom." Alison's voice drew her attention away from the shop window. "We were just on our way to meet you. What are you doing?"

Turning, Edie noticed that Alison seemed particularly vivacious, all radiant and fresh with an extra sparkle in her brown eyes. Jerry was with her, a typical hint of a smile in his expression.

"I was just admiring the dress in the window," Edie admitted. "Isn't it attractive?"

"It's gorgeous! It would look great on you, mom," Alison insisted the instant she saw it. "You should get it."

"And where would I wear it?" Edie shook her head, too practical to buy something that would end up hanging in her closet. "What I need is a new pair of jeans. I would get a lot more use out of those than I would that dress, beautiful as it is."

"It is attractive," Jerry agreed with their consensus.

"And you could wear it to the dance tonight," Alison inserted.

"What dance?" It was the first time Edie had heard anything mentioned about a dance. Her gaze darted curiously to her daughter.

"Jerry and I had some time to kill before meeting you so we stopped at this bar," Alison began.

Jerry interrupted to assure Edie, "I had a beer and Alison had a Coke."

"Yes, well," Alison hurried on with her explanation, "since it's Saturday night, they have a band coming in to play at this bar. Rob says they're really good. He's heard them play before."

"Who is Rob?" Edie frowned in amusement.

"He's this really cute cowboy who was in the bar the same time we were there." That explained the excited glow in her eyes.

"And this 'really cute' cowboy asked her if she was going to come to the dance tonight and made her promise to save a dance for him," Jerry teasingly carried the explanation a step further.

"I think I get the picture now," Edie laughed.

Alison looked self-conscious for only an instant before she shrugged it off. "He might change his mind and not even be there tonight. But I still think we should go to the dance. We've all worked hard lately. It's time we had a night on the town."

"I agree," Edie said. "But I don't need to buy a new dress to go to a dance."

"You haven't had a new dress in years, at least not one like that." Alison glanced again at the dress on the mannequin. "Let's go in and see if they have it in your size." She grabbed Edie's arm to pull her into the shop. "There wouldn't be any harm in trying it on. You might look terrible in it—who knows?"

When the clerk informed them they did have the dress in Edie's size, Alison took the packages from her arms and thrust them into Jerry's. Edie wasn't given a chance to resist as she and the dress were hustled into a fitting room to change.

Everything was perfect—the length, the fit, the color, everything. She wasn't able to fasten the hook above the back zipper, but it didn't alter the appearance of the dress. She emerged from the dressing room, minus any shoes since her cowboy boots had looked absurd, to view herself in the full-length mirror.

Alison was busy looking through a rack of dresses with Jerry standing patiently to one side. She didn't notice Edie when she came out of the fitting room, and Edie didn't immediately try to attract their attention, too anxious to see if the dress looked as good as it felt.

For an instant she was dazed by the image of a slim, fully curved woman with burnished brown hair. The dress enhanced a natural allure Edie hadn't realized she possessed. It was as if she was discovering all over again that she was a woman...and liking the sensation. With a three-quarter turn she looked over her shoulder into the mirror to get a back view of the dress. Standing on tiptoes, she tried to get an idea of what the dress would look like with heels. Out of the corner of her eye she glimpsed the distinctive rolled brim of a cowboy hat. Automatically Edie assumed Jerry had noticed her and had walked over for a closer look. She reached behind her back with one hand to try to reach the unfastened hook.

"I wasn't able to fasten the hook but—" It didn't detract that much from the appearance. The material above the zipper simply didn't lie as smooth against her skin as it could. "What do you think?"

"I think it's a sin that a body like that spends so much time in men's clothes." The caressingly low pitch of Maddock's voice paralyzed Edie.

Her heart leaped into her throat, robbing her of even the ability to speak. There was movement as the reflection of his tall, muscled lines joined hers in the mirror. "Let me get that hook for you."

The pleasant roughness of his fingers touched the bare skin of her backbone just above the zipper. The vibrations they produced shook Edie out of her trance.

"No. It isn't necessary." She would have stepped away from him, but he already had a hold on the material of her dress. Knowing his strength and the fragility of the fabric, she didn't try to pull away and risk tearing the material.

"A man learns early in his life the mysteries of all the hooks, snaps and zippers that clutter women's clothes," he murmured in dry insinuation.

"Were you a slow learner? You seem to be having difficulty with that hook." Edie was having difficulty keeping her breathlessness out of her voice.

"The adeptness comes in undoing them. There isn't any need to hurry when a man is re-fastening a hook," Maddock informed her smoothly, as if aware of the effect his touch was having on her.

It was a combination of his touch and the task. There was something about having a man fasten a dress that made it heavy with implied intimacy. Edie's senses were reacting to that feeling. When he had finished, Maddock turned her to face the mirror. Their gazes locked in the reflecting glass. His lazy gray eyes took note of the wary and disturbed darkness of hers, while Edie tried not to be aware of the way his figure-molding clothes enhanced his attraction. The tempo of her pulse went out of control when he made a leisurely inspection of her length.

"A pair of shoes would add the finishing touch to the dress," he observed dryly. The remark pulled her gaze from his tanned features, so masculine and tough, so disturbingly attractive, to the bareness of her own feet. "Don't you agree, Felicia?"

The mention of his daughter's name jerked Edie's gaze to the side where she encountered the brunette girl's cold regard. For a fleeting second Edie was surprised to see jealousy and resentment smoldering in Felicia's expression before it was disguised with a look of boredom.

"It would be an improvement," Felicia agreed with marked indifference.

"Mother! You look stunning!" Alison declared in a breathy exclamation when she noticed Edie standing in front of the mirror and moved away from the dress rack for a closer look. "Doesn't she, Jerry?"

"It's beautiful, Edie." His agreement was restrained but no less sincere as his attention was drawn to Felicia Maddock.

"I thought you were in such a hurry to get

back to the ranch," the brunette accused with an attempt at hauteur.

"I don't recall saying that," Jerry denied quietly but firmly.

With a sidelong look through her lashes, Edie glanced at Maddock to see if he was observing this duel of wills between her stepson and his daughter. He was watching them, all right, but the instant she looked at him his gaze dropped to meet hers. She glimpsed the light of challenge in his gray depths, but didn't understand its cause.

"I had a skirt that was being altered. Daddy and I stopped by to pick it up," Felicia explained quickly, as if she didn't want Jerry to think she had followed him into the store.

"It fits you perfectly, mom. You don't have to do a thing to it." Alison shook her head in amazement. "It's even the right length. Turn around so I can see the back."

Edie pivoted self-consciously, aware that her daughter wasn't the only one showing a lot of interest in the way the dress fit her. She was shaken by the sensation that she was modeling it for Maddock's benefit, seeking his approval. His gaze seemed to mock her with the knowledge when she unwillingly met it.

"You've got to buy it and wear it to the dance tonight," Alison insisted.

She felt the faint narrowing of interest in Maddock's look. Her throat became tight, nerves tensing. "No," Edie said, and raised a hand in a shielding gesture to lift the curtain of hair near her ear. "What I mean is . . . I don't think I'll go to the dance, so I don't need this dress. You and Jerry can go, but I'll stay home."

"You will not," Alison protested with an irritated frown, and turned to her half-brother for help. "Jerry, talk to her."

"We've all been working hard, Edie. You need to go out tonight and have fun as much as we do," he insisted quietly.

"We'll talk about it later." Edie moved away from the mirror . . . and Maddock. She tried to sound light and uncaring as if it was all unimportant.

"Miss?" Jerry motioned to the sales clerk for her attention. "We'll buy this dress."

"Jerry—" Her voice was low and vibrating with impatience.

But he was too old to be silenced by the angry sparks in her eyes. The faint smile in his maturing face told her so.

"When was the last time you went dancing, Edie?" Jerry questioned and immediately provided an answer. "It had to be before you married dad, because he had two left feet and nobody could drag him onto the dance floor. We all had to gang up on him just to persuade him to take us out to dinner."

Again she glanced at Maddock, who was listening without any qualms. Jerry's statement made Joe sound as if he hadn't been a very loving husband. She felt duty bound to defend him.

"I didn't mind," she reminded Jerry.

"I know you didn't mind. That was dad. We all loved him for what he was, not what he did or didn't do. I'm only saying it's time you had fun," Jerry replied. "And don't say you don't know how to dance, because you are the one who taught me."

"I just don't feel like going." It was a weak excuse no matter how stiffly she issued it.

"Okay." Jerry shrugged an acceptance. "If you are going to stay home, Alison and I will, too."

"Jerry," Alison wailed in protest.

"You are both old enough to do what you want. You don't need me along." Edie felt she was being unfairly pressured.

"If you don't go, we don't go," Jerry repeated, and glanced at his half-sister. "Agreed?"

A long, defeated sigh came from Alison as she nodded a reluctant, "Agreed."

"That is blackmail, Jerry Gibbs," Edie accused. "Emotional blackmail."

"I think that's what it is," he agreed with an impudent grin.

"Does that mean we're going?" Holding her breath, Alison glanced eagerly from one to the other.

"Yes." Edie grudgingly gave in to the pressure.

"Oh, good! I found this darling yellow pantsuit, mom. Let me show it to you." Alison dashed back to the rack. "I thought I'd treat myself to a new outfit, too."

The sales clerk passed in front of Edie to hand a package to Felicia Maddock. "I'm sorry you had to wait so long, Miss Maddock," the clerk apologized. "The alterations to your skirt took a little longer than we anticipated."

"That's quite all right." There was a briskness of dismissal in the reply as Felicia glanced over her shoulder. "Are you ready, daddy?"

"Whenever you are," he agreed blandly, but Edie thought she noticed a flicker of irritation in his expression.

His daughter paused to flash an aloof smile at Jerry. "Maybe we'll see you at the dance tonight. Daddy and I have been talking about going. He doesn't like me to go alone because sometimes it gets a little rough in places like that. You could ride in with us if you like. It wouldn't be out of our way to stop by your place," she offered.

Jerry was already shaking his head in refusal. Before he could voice it, Maddock was at his daughter's side, taking her arm. "I haven't decided that we're going tonight, Felicia," he stated.

Relief trembled through Edie. The prospect of Maddock attending the dance had filled her with all sorts of misgivings. Now it seemed likely he wouldn't be there, or he wouldn't have corrected his daughter. Edie wondered whether he was refusing because he didn't want his daughter chasing Jerry, or if it was because he wasn't interested in running into her.

Felicia appeared unperturbed by his statement, although she surrendered to the pressure of his guiding hand. She smiled over her shoulder at Jerry. "We'll see you tonight," she said confidently.

As Maddock escorted her out of the shop, Jerry murmured, "He should make her stay home on general principles."

"I pity your kids, Jerry," Alison declared. "You are going to be a strict father." She held up the pantsuit for Edie's inspection. "What do you think of it, mom?"

"It looks great on the hanger. Why don't you try it on while I change out of this dress?" Edie suggested.

"Do you like it, mean Daddy Jerry?" Alison teased him again about his sternness.

"Yes, I like it," he agreed absently while sending her a sharp look. "And I'm not being too strict. I just know our kids aren't going to turn out like Felicia—pampered and spoiled."

"*Our* kids?" Edie raised an eyebrow in curious surprise.

It had been years since she'd seen Jerry blush—not since his early teenage years. But a scarlet red was now spreading up from his neck to flame his face.

"I meant...when Alison has kids, and I have

kids—our kids—we won't spoil them,'' he tried to bluff his way out of that slip.

But Edie knew that wasn't what he'd meant at all. When he had said "our" he had been referring to Felicia and himself. She felt a quiet rage searing through her. What was it about these Maddocks that could make you criticize them, find fault with them, dislike them even, and yet be so inexplicably drawn to them.

But all this escaped Alison's notice. "You're right, Jerry. If any kid of mine started acting like that brat, I'd make sure they didn't sit down for a week." She hugged the pantsuit to her. "I'm going to go try this on."

Edie followed her to the dressing room to change back into her slacks and top and put her boots on. She pretended to accept Jerry's explanation for the time being. After all, who was she to give advice when she couldn't control her own wayward thoughts?

The only thing that needed to be done to Alison's pantsuit was shorten the legs the width of the hem. The shop wasn't able to make the alteration in time for Alison to wear it to the dance that night, so Edie agreed to do it when they got home.

By the time they had lunch, did their grocery shopping and drove to the ranch, it was time to start choring. Chaos set in as they tried to fix supper, eat it, shorten the pantsuit, take baths and get ready.

Edie was taking the last stitch in the hem of

the slacks when Alison rushed into the room in her bathrobe. "Mom, help me! I washed my hair and now I can't do a thing with it!" The styling dryer was in one hand, a brush and curling wand in the other.

"How long is this going to take?" Jerry asked with a sigh. Already dressed in a casual forest-green suit, he was sitting on the couch, twirling his hat in his hand in an attempt at patience.

"You. can't expect me to go looking like this," Alison defended.

"It wouldn't make a very good impression on that cute cowboy, Rob, would it?" he grinned. She wrinkled her nose at him then laughed. "Edie still has to get dressed and you still have to put your makeup on. I'm going to go to sleep waiting for you guys." He straightened. "If it's okay, I'm going into town now. You guys can drive the car. I'll take the truck."

"Go on ahead," Edie agreed and knotted the hem thread. "It may take us a while."

"If you don't come with Alison, I'll drive back out here for you," Jerry warned.

"I'll be there," she promised.

"Save us a table," Alison called after him as he walked to the door.

"If you aren't there by midnight, the table is liable to turn into a pumpkin." Then the door was slamming behind him.

It was nearly an hour later before they left the ranch. The late-setting summer sun was just dipping below the horizon when they reached the outskirts of Custer. There wasn't any place to park near the bar, but they finally found a spot more than a block away.

The bar was typically dimly lighted and crowded with people. Amplifiers, positioned strategically throughout the room, blared with the country music being played by the band on the small stage. Jerry saw them before they even noticed him in the multitude of people. As Edie wound her way through the maze of tables and chairs ahead of Alison to the one near the dance floor, she realized there was another man with Jerry. Alison was quick to identify him as Rob Lydell, her cowboy.

"We were just about to send out a search party for you two," Jerry shouted above the din of music and voices, then managed an introduction to the young but sun-aged cowboy who possessed an engaging smile.

The waitress stopped at their table. Jerry and Rob ordered two more beers, but Edie elected to have a Coke, as did Alison. At first it was difficult to hear the conversation, but she gradually learned to siphon out the other sounds and listen only to those at her table. They laughed and talked, then Rob asked Alison to dance.

"He seems nice," Edie observed as she watched the pair circling the crowded dance floor.

"I like him—which is more than I could say for some of Alison's choices," Jerry agreed with a rueful smile. "Like lover boy Craig."

"I try not to remember him," Edie murmured.

When the band finished the ballad they went immediately into an up-tempo tune. The couple stayed on the floor to dance to it. After that song was over the band took a twenty-minute break. Edie tried not to notice that Rob's chair had slid closer to Alison's when they came back to sit at the table.

Some of Rob's friends stopped by to talk as a jukebox took over for the band. Edie was glad that they had come to the dance. Jerry and Alison were meeting more people in this one night than they had met since they had moved here. They should have begun socializing sooner, except there had been so much work to do.

As the band returned to the small stage after their break, Edie leaned forward to mention her thought to Jerry. His attention was focused on the dance floor when he suddenly looked very tense. He appeared to force himself to relax. Curious, Edie followed the direction of his gaze and saw Felicia Maddock dancing with some cowboy. At that moment the brunette glanced toward their table and feigned a look of surprise.

"Hi, Jerry!" She waved and smiled a greeting that was much too casual. "I told you I would see you tonight." Then she was being whirled into the center of the floor by her partner.

"Little Miss Nose-in-the-air can't even say hello to me," Alison grumbled in irritation.

"She's like that sometimes," Rob admitted, "but she isn't really a bad kid." As if he realized his opinion didn't exactly please Alison, he let the subject drop.

Jerry made no comment, although Edie noticed his gaze kept straying to the dance floor, keeping track of the young brunette. But he wasn't nearly as talkative as he had been before. For that matter, neither was she. If Felicia was here, so was Maddock. Unconsciously, Edie kept searching for him until she saw him standing at the counter bar.

There was an understated simplicity to his clothes—a white shirt unbuttoned at the throat and a buckskin vest hanging open. The western cut of his brown slacks fitted closely to his hips and legs, flaring slightly over his boots with their underslung rider's heels. He was engaged in conversation with a cowboy standing beside him. When his head turned in the direction of the dance floor, Edie looked immediately away, not wanting to be caught looking at him.

Aware of his presence, it was impossible to keep her gaze from straying to him. Yet Maddock didn't seem to notice her at all. She did a poor job of convincing herself that she was glad.

Alison was in high spirits as she returned to the table hand in hand with her cowboy. Her face was aglow. To Edie her daughter seemed to be floating on air. She felt a tad bit envious when Alison drifted to the chair beside her.

Rob didn't immediately sit down. "Want another beer, Jerry?"

Jerry seemed to have a hard time assimilating the question, not answering until he had torn his gaze from the couples leaving the dance floor. "Yeah, I'll have another," he agreed while drawing a deep breath.

"Would you like another Coke, Alison?" Rob inquired, and received an affirmative and smiling nod. His glance then sought out Edie. "How about you, Mrs. Gibbs?"

The appellation made her feel extraordinarily old. "No, thank you," she refused.

The cowboy had barely left the table before Alison was leaning excitedly toward her. "Rob wants to take me home. Do you think it's all right, mom?"

"I just met him, Alison," Edie protested. "I don't know anything about him. Neither do you."

"He's nice. You can see that." Alison was at her persuasive best. "What shall I tell him?"

Maternal instinct insisted that Edie order Alison to come home with her, but it was overwhelmed by the memory of Rob's voice referring to her as Mrs. Gibbs. Her sigh was almost inaudible.

"I can't give you an answer just yet. You can't expect me to make a spur-of-the-moment decision like that, Alison. Let me think about it," she insisted with a vague smile of reassurance.

"But what if he asks me?" her daughter frowned anxiously.

"Let him dangle a little," Edie shrugged. "Tell him that he'll have to wait and see."

With a grimacing sigh, Alison straightened to glance at the returning cowboy and smile a quick welcome. Edie inspected Rob with a closer eye. Her conclusion matched Jerry's. Rob Lydell was an improvement on some of Alison's past choices in boyfriends.

She didn't notice Jerry rise to his feet until he touched her arm. "The band is playing a slow song, Edie. Want to dance?"

"I'd love to," she agreed without hesitation, and straightened from her chair. "It's been ages since I've danced, so if I step on your toes, don't complain," she added as Jerry guided her onto the dance floor.

"I'm not worried about you stepping on my toes," he grinned. "After all, you're the one that taught both me and Alison how to dance." He turned her into his arms.

CHAPTER NINE

WITHIN SECONDS after they had joined the other couples on the dance floor, Jerry became silent and his expression grew serious. Edie glanced around to find the source of his distraction. She knew she had located it the instant her gaze found Felicia dancing with her father. Edie looked quickly away, but not before her heart did a succession of flips at the sight of Will Maddock.

All her senses were on guard, alerted now to the rancher's presence and tracking him with some built-in kind of radar. When someone brushed a shoulder against hers, Edie didn't have to turn to know who it was.

Confirmation came with the stiffening of Jerry's arm around her waist and the low pitch of Will Maddock's familiar voice as he suggested, "Why don't we change partners?"

Edie couldn't think of a single, logical reason to refuse, especially when Jerry was releasing her to welcome Felicia. Then Will's large hand was on her waist, and Edie found herself being guided into his arms and matching her steps to the simple pattern of his. When she lifted her gaze to his rugged face, his gray eyes were smiling at her in a knowing fashion, as if aware of the disturbing effect he had on her. Yet Edie suspected it was all her imagination.

When his gaze drifted after the couple dancing away from them, she glanced at them, too. The young pair were completely wrapped up in each other, oblivious to everything else around them.

"Young love." There was a dryness to Will's remark, and it glittered in his eyes when Edie glanced at them. "No one could pay me to go through those throes of agony again."

In spite of herself she smiled. "Neither would I." She was conscious of a very comfortable closeness, something warm and wonderful.

"My daughter is a true Maddock," he observed in the same tone as before. "Once she decides she wants something, she goes after it. I'm afraid she has decided she wants your stepson."

"Jerry is of the opinion that she has some growing up to do," Edie replied. "At the moment he finds her spoiled, self-centered and immature."

There was agreement in his throaty chuckle. "I always believed that boy had a head on his shoulders, even if he is caught up in that dream of yours about the ranch." Before Edie could take offense at his remark, Will Maddock continued. "That's the trouble with being an only parent. It's hard to say no. I keep trying to make up for the fact that she doesn't have a mother. Normally I wouldn't approve of Felicia being with someone Jerry's age, but I'm hoping he will gently teach her that she can't always have her way."

Her arm tightened around her waist as he avoided a collision with another couple. It broke the pattern and Edie missed a step and brushed against him. The contact with the hard-muscled flesh of his body brought an instant recall of other times when she had been held this close. She had accepted the fact that she found him sexually attractive, but she was only just beginning to discover that he aroused her emotionally, too. Its existence was strong at this moment as his hand shaped itself to the small of her back.

She resisted the molding pressure of his hand as she resisted the discovery of her growing emotional involvement. Directing her gaze away from the broad set of his shoulders and the tanned column of his throat, she sought the distraction of other couples on the dance floor. Alison was among them, her arms wrapped around the neck of her partner.

"Maddock, do you know anything about that cowboy dancing with Alison?" She drew his attention to the pair. "His name is Rob Lydell."

"Yes, I know him. What about him?" His glance was curious.

"He has asked to give Alison a ride home tonight," she explained. "I've only just met him, and I wasn't sure whether I should let Alison go with him or not.''

The corners of his mouth twitched in an attempt to suppress a smile. ''I think it's safe to say you can trust him.'' His tone and his vaguely amused attitude caused Edie to frown in confusion. ''Rob works for me,'' he revealed. At first she was too stunned by his answer to reply.

''I should have guessed,'' she murmured almost under her breath. What was there about these Maddocks, she wondered. First Jerry was succumbing to his daughter's charm, and Alison was all wrapped up with one of his hired hands. And here she was, caught up in some crazy longing for the rancher himself.

''If you'd like, I'll have a talk with Rob and make certain you have no cause for concern about Alison,'' he offered with parental understanding.

''It isn't that.'' She shook her head, impatient and suddenly defensive. She attacked out of instinct. ''Why can't you leave us alone?''

His glinting gray eyes ran over her face, following her thoughts. The line of his mouth became mocking. ''You know the old saying—if you can't beat them, join them.''

It wasn't meant to be taken seriously, she realized. He was only baiting her, trying to get a rise from her. Well, she wasn't going to give him the satisfaction. Her gaze was fixed on a point beyond his shoulder. Maddock uncurled his fingers from around her head and tucked one under her chin, lifting it. She was forced to meet his steady gray eyes.

"We Maddocks aren't such a bad lot, Edie. You've got the wrong impression of us altogether," he murmured. "Our differences have been on a purely business level. Your mistake was taking it personally. I've told you that before, but you still don't believe me. Your ranch happens to sit on land I want. If you had bought any other place, I would have wished you the best of luck."

His fingers slowly stroked the underside of her jaw, tracing its firm set. Edie closed her eyes at the raw ache his caress induced. Her fingers closed over his forearm to draw his hand away as the music stopped.

"Which doesn't change the fact that we still own the ranch, Maddock, and we aren't going to sell it to anyone," she replied tightly.

Turning out of his arm, she left the dance floor to return to her table. She was conscious that he followed her, escorting her back. At the table he pulled out her chair. As she sat down, both Jerry and Alison returned. She looked up to see the measured look Maddock gave the two before he nodded briefly to her and moved away toward the bar.

"You didn't mind changing partners, did you, Edie?" Jerry studied the stillness of her features with an anxious frown.

"Of course not." Her assuring smile was stiff, not fully natural.

But Jerry didn't seem to notice as his gaze traveled after the rancher, seeking him out among the others lined up at the bar. "What do you think Maddock would say if I asked to take Felicia home?"

"I'm sure you would have his permission," she replied, remembering the approval Maddock had voiced about Jerry.

"Did he say anything about Felicia and me while you were dancing?" Jerry was quick to catch the note of certainty in her tone.

"Yes. Something to the effect that Felicia has made up her mind she wants you...and a Maddock always gets what he or she wants. So I don't think your request will come as any surprise to him." She smiled to take the little sting of bitterness out of her words.

But Jerry hadn't noticed it. "Excuse me." He rose from his chair to make his way through the crowd to Felicia.

"I don't know what he sees in her," Alison muttered. "She's a brat."

"But a very beautiful brat," Edie pointed out, then remarked on the absence of her daughter's suitor. "Where is Rob?"

"He stopped to chat with some friends. He'll be here shortly," Alison replied confidently.

"You didn't mention that he worked for Maddock." Edie observed the way her daughter nibbled at her lip, revealing the information had been known to her.

"Just because he works for them doesn't

make him like them," she reasoned. "Rob is nice."

"I'm not going to argue with that. If you want to ride home with him, I have no objection." After all, Maddock had vouched for him and it was obviously what Alison wanted.

"Thanks, mom." Her face was wreathed by a smile as she leaned over to give Edie a quick hug.

Rob returned to the table to sit beside Alison, and Edie was forgotten as the two spoke in low voices to each other. With Jerry gone as well, Edie felt superfluous. Everyone was paired up except her, and she didn't like the lonely feeling that gave her.

Rising, she laid a hand on her daughter's shoulder to gently intrude on their conversation. "I'm going home," she explained as the reason for the interruption.

"You can't leave now, mom," Alison protested. "It's early yet."

"Maybe for you, but it's late for me." She glanced at the young man sitting so close to her daughter and smiled. "Good night, Rob."

"Good night, ma'am. I'll see that Alison gets home safely," he promised.

"I won't be late," Alison added.

"Tell Jerry I've left when you see him," Edie said as she moved away from the table toward the door.

Outside, the music and the noise of the bar was muffled. Edie paused and lifted her gaze to the night sky, brilliant with stars. A big, heavy moon lolled above the jagged horizon of the Black Hills. After the smoke-filled bar, the air smelled fresh and sweet.

As her thoughts wandered over the night's events, she strolled in the direction of the parked car. What was it the master battle tacticians said? Divide and conquer. That was precisely what was happening. Jerry was with Felicia Maddock. Alison was with Rob Lydell, Maddock's hired man. And she was finding Maddock more irresistible with each meeting. It didn't bode well for the future.

She sighed and crossed in front of the dark opening to an alleyway. With her head down, Edie didn't notice the next building contained a honky-tonk bar until the door slammed and three laughing cowboys staggered outside. They dawdled there, trying to decide where to go next. They were blocking the front part of the sidewalk, so Edie moved to walk behind them and continue to her car parked half a block away. At that moment they noticed her, and one of them let out a long wolf whistle. The implied compliment tugged at the corners of her mouth with a smile.

"Where are you going, honey?" One of the young cowboys moved in front of her to stop her.

"Can we come along?" a second spoke up.

The building was at her back as they crowded around her, yet there was nothing threatening in their manner. They'd had a few drinks and were ready for a good time. Edie was neither worried nor afraid.

"Sorry, fellas. I'm on my way home, so how about letting me by?" Her request was friendly but firm.

"The night's young," the third insisted. "It's too early to go home."

"I'll bet she had a fight with her boyfriend," the first one guessed.

The second cowboy took up the thought before Edie could respond. "You aren't going to let him spoil your evening, are you? It would be a shame to let that pretty dress go to waste."

"We'll take you out," the first one offered. "You just tell us where you want to go and we'll take you." There was a chorus of agreement from the other two.

"Thanks for the invitation, but I want to go home—*alone*." She stressed the last to leave them in no doubt. "Would you mind letting me pass?"

There was a slight shift, creating a gap between two of them. As Edie started to slip through it, the third cowboy made one last attempt to change her mind.

"Come on, honey. Take pity on three lonely cowboys," he coaxed.

A voice came from behind all of them. "You boys aren't listening. The lady said no."

Edie pivoted as she recognized Will Maddock's voice. The sight of his large frame stand-

ing by the shadows of the alleyway took everyone by surprise. The young cowboy closest to
him recovered first and swaggered forward a
couple of steps.

"Well, well, well. If it ain't the big bull of the
woods himself," he drawled with exaggerated
thickness. "I don't recall you bein' invited to
this party."

"I invited myself. Now let the lady pass."
There was a steel-hard quality to his voice, but
his face was in the shadows and Edie couldn't
make out his features.

The third cowboy continued to stand in front
of Maddock in silent challenge. "Is that an
order?"

"Yes."

Edie felt the tension build in the air. These
boys were ripe for some excitement, and Maddock's attitude was all the provocation they
needed. She could sense it rippling through the
trio of cowhands out for a night on the town.

"What if we don't obey your order?" the
freckle-faced one on Edie's left inquired with
feigned innocence.

"I guess I'll have to show you that it's the
right thing to do." Maddock shrugged easily.

"Maddock—" She attempted to protest his
handling of the situation, but he didn't give her
a chance.

"Stay out of this, Edie," he ordered tersely.

"Edie?" The second cowboy looked at her,
catching Maddock's familiar use of her name

and drawing his own conclusion. "Is he the one who spoiled your evening and sent you home early?"

She intended to respond to that and attempt to defuse the scene, but it had already escalated beyond the point where any of the men would listen to her. She realized that as soon as the first cowboy took a step toward Maddock.

"I always wondered if you were as tough as everyone says," he murmured. "I guess I'll have to find out for myself."

"I guess you will," Maddock agreed.

The cowboy took the first swing, a blow that was warded off by Maddock's upraised arm. With every intention of stopping the fight before it went further, Edie took a step forward, but the shortest cowboy of the trio caught her by the waist to prevent her from reaching the scuffling pair.

"You'd better stay here, miss," he advised for her own protection. "We don't want you getting hurt."

Despite her struggles, she was held fast. When it became apparent that the first cowboy was getting the worst of it, the freckle-faced cowboy rushed in to help his buddy. The cowboy holding Edie blocked most of her view, limiting her knowledge of the fight to the grunting sounds of the protagonists, the thud of landing fists and thrashing bodies.

Finally there was a kind of silence underlined with heavy breathing and punctuated with soft

moans. The arms holding Edie loosened as the
last cowboy carefully let her go and moved out of
her way. She saw Maddock standing there,
breathing hard and swaying a little while his two
opponents staggered unsteadily to their feet.

"Had enough?" His rough voice made a winded challenge.

One of them nodded an affirmative answer
and reached down to scoop up Maddock's hat
and hand it to him. Edie stared in stunned disbelief as the cowboy's hand remained outstretched
to shake Maddock's. The second cowboy did the
same in a show of no hard feelings. Then all three
were drifting across the street. Edie heard the
good-natured ribbing start among them before
they reached the other side.

"Are you all right?"

Maddock's question roused her from her stillness. Men, she thought, why do they think everything has to be settled by a fight?

"Who asked you to interfere?" she demanded, because as far as she was concerned, she
hadn't been in any danger at all. The resulting
brawl had been completely unnecessary.

"No one. The boys were looking for some
adventure. It's better that I supplied it instead of
you," he said, straightening a little and squaring
his shoulders as if regathering his strength.

Her gaze narrowed in sharp suspicion as it occurred to her that Maddock had not simply
"happened" to come this way. "Why were you
following me?"

"I realized that I hadn't told you how attractive your dress is with shoes." His compliment reminded her of that afternoon when he'd seen her trying on the dress barefoot. Some of her irritation faded with his remark. He lifted a hand to his cheek and wiped at it. She saw the glistening dark stain of blood on his fingers. "One of those damned cowboys cut me with a ring," he muttered under his breath.

"You'd better let me look at it." She walked over to him and took the handkerchief he produced from a rear pocket. Folding it, she dabbed at the blood oozing from the gash on his cheekbone. In the shadowed night she couldn't tell the extent of the injury. "There isn't enough light here."

"There's a back entrance to this bar in the alley. The owner is a friend of mine. We can use his office in the rear." With the first step he took toward the dark alley, he swayed unsteadily. Edie was instantly at his side to curve an arm around his middle, offering him slim support. Maddock paused, leaning some of his weight on her until his legs were steady under him. He draped an arm across her shoulders, his hand closing on the soft flesh of her arm, and started into the alley. "I haven't been in a fight for five years. If that third man had come at me, I don't think I would have been standing at the end."

"There wasn't any reason for that fight," Edie remembered in a surge of impatience. "They were letting me go when you showed up."

"It didn't look that way to me." The darkness of the alley enveloped them, and Maddock made his way to the rear door by instinct alone. "Either way, it's spilled milk now." He rapped on the wooden door.

"As usual a woman has to clean up the mess," she murmured with the sharp edge of her tongue.

"As usual she does." His soft chuckle mocked her irritated response.

The door was opened by a portly, balding man in a tightly collared shirt with a string tie. His frowning glance widened to an open stare of shock as the interior light illuminated Maddock's face.

"It isn't as bad as it looks, Tubby," Maddock assured the man in a dryly weary voice. But Edie felt the same start of shock at the smeared blood and purpling flesh around his cheekbone and jaw. She had taken care of too many of her children's cuts and bruises not to realize that Maddock's assessment was probably accurate.

"Come in, Will." The owner opened the door wider to admit them. "Sit here in my office and I'll get a wet cloth and the first-aid box."

The stout man disappeared, leaving the private office through an interior door where the sounds of loud voices and a jukebox filtered into the room. Edie helped Maddock into a straight-backed chair beside the desk littered with papers, rolls of register tape and delivery slips. Within seconds the owner returned with a clean, wet cloth and the first-aid kit. Edie took the cloth and knelt down to begin carefully wiping the blood smears from Maddock's face. The owner hovered beside her, gritting his teeth and making faces as if he was the patient.

"Do you think that cut will need stitches?" he asked. "Maybe I should call a doctor?"

The wound had already stopped bleeding. Edie studied it carefully. "It isn't as deep as it looks. I don't think it will need stitches," she concluded, but she was well aware that if it had been half an inch higher, it would have been his eye that was cut. Her concern was overridden by irritation at his senseless risk that could have resulted in permanent injury. Her mouth thinned into a grimly angry line.

"Is there anything else I can do?" the owner offered. "Anything you need?"

"I think we can manage alone," Maddock replied. "Thanks, Tubby."

"I'll go out front and give Mike a hand at the bar. If you need me, just shout," the man insisted.

"We will." After the door latch had clicked shut, Maddock caught her eye with a glinting look. "The poor guy can't stand the sight of blood."

"It's a shame you don't suffer from the same problem. Maybe you wouldn't have ended up looking like this." Her glance slashed over his face. There hadn't been as much damage as it had first appeared. Except for the gash on his cheekbone, there was a bruise along his jaw and a purpling area near the cut. It could easily have been much worse.

Setting the stained, wet cloth aside, Edie opened the first-aid kit and removed a bottle of iodine. She used the applicator attached to the lid and dabbed some of the antiseptic into a corner of his wound. Maddock breathed in with a sharp, hissing sound and recoiled.

"Hold still," she ordered without sympathy, and applied more iodine.

"Ouch!"

"I'd like to know what it is about iodine that can turn grown men into little boys—the same grown men that take fists in their face without a whimper," she mocked him with a trace of acidity.

His gray eyes danced wickedly, not taking offense as they met her look. "Maybe I'm missing the soothing hand on my brow."

"You're getting just what you deserve." She added an extra amount of iodine to what had already been applied.

"I was under the impression that a woman liked to have men fight over her," he mocked.

"Not this woman," Edie retorted. "I don't think it ever occurred to you that someone could have been seriously hurt. You could have injured your eye, possibly lost the sight in it." She recapped the iodine bottle and straightened to return it to the first-aid kit.

Maddock caught her wrist and turned her around to face him as his strong features tilted up to view her expression. His steady gaze seemed to penetrate behind her mask of irritation.

"I was beginning to think you didn't care," he murmured.

"It was stupid of you to fight." She found it difficult to retain her lack of patience with him. "You're too old for that sort of thing."

"Too old?" He laughed heartily and pulled her onto his lap. "I come to the aid of a damsel in distress and she accuses me of being *too old*!"

"I didn't mean it that way," she protested. How could she when she was so fully aware of the powerful strength of his arms encircling her and his potent male vitality. The heat of his body was already stealing the force of her anger and kindling an entirely different response. "I meant you should have had more sense."

"Where you're concerned, Edie, I seem to have lost all ability to reason," he murmured, and narrowed the distance between their lips until she felt the warmth of his breath against her skin. "Hadn't you noticed?"

"No," she whispered.

As his mouth settled onto her lips in a deep, searching kiss, her eyes closed and her arms found their way around his neck. In his arms she found the fulfillment her heart had been seeking. Emotion swelled within her in a floodtide of intense longing.

His hand roamed over her stomach and ribs

and burned through the soft fabric covering her breast. Tremors of desire quivered through her, caused by his caress. The driving pressure of his kiss told of his need, assuring her that she was not alone in this golden spiral of feelings.

There was a rough possession in the kisses he burned into her face and neck, claiming every inch of her. "I'm not convinced anymore that any man can arouse you like this, Edie," he murmured thickly. "You are showing me more than a purely sexual response."

She rubbed her lips against his throat, savoring the taste of his skin. "I'm not sure what I'm thinking or feeling." With each drumming beat of her heart, she was becoming more sure of the love growing inside her for this man, but she kept it silent, betraying it not by word but by deed.

Maddock sighed and reluctantly lifted his head. His gray eyes smoldered with barely disguised impatience and desire, yet his actions were controlled. He removed his hand from her breast and forced it to wander restlessly to her shoulder.

"Tubby will be coming back to see how we're doing," he answered the question that was in her eyes. "I think we should leave."

"Yes," she agreed, and let him help her off his lap. "It's time I was going home." She was disappointed when Maddock failed to make an alternative suggestion.

"I'll walk you to your car," was his only offer.

Edie waited by the back door while Maddock let the owner know they were leaving and thanked him for the help. He took her hand to lead her out of the alley to the lighted street and walked with her the half block to her car. He opened the driver's door for her and waited until she was behind the wheel to shut it.

"My car is parked around the corner," he said. "I'll follow you to make sure you get home in one piece."

"Okay." She smiled an instant agreement, glad that she hadn't seen the last of him this night.

Shortly after Edie pulled onto the highway, she saw the headlights of Maddock's car reflected in her rearview mirror. It made her feel warm and wanted inside. All her adult life she had been the one who looked after others. It was a novel experience to have someone looking after her. She rather liked the feeling.

The drive to the ranch didn't seem as long with his headlights winking in her mirror. There was a soft curve to her lips as she stopped the car in front of the house and climbed out. She waited for Maddock while he parked behind her car and stepped out.

"Would you like to come in for coffee?" she invited as he approached. "It won't take long to fix some."

"I was hoping you'd ask," he replied, and took her arm as they climbed the porch steps to the front door.

Once inside, Edie paused to turn on a light.

"Make yourself comfortable while I go to the kitchen and fix the coffee."

She had already started in that direction when Maddock called her name quietly yet insistently. "Edie?"

She stopped and half turned. "Yes?"

He walked up to her and stopped. "Coffee was just an excuse. We both know that."

Her pulse accelerated its tempo and she suddenly had difficulty breathing. All conscious thought was swept aside by the dark intensity of his gray eyes, urgent and compelling. His hands curved onto the soft curves of her shoulders, applying pressure to draw her toward him. The moment became prolonged as he slowly bent his head and nuzzled the sensitive curve of her neck. A sigh of aching pleasure whispered from her lips.

She was absently amazed that someone so powerfully built could be so gentle yet firm. But Maddock seemed to be made from a series of contradictions. Here was a man strong enough to be gentle, ruthless enough to be kind and arrogant enough to be vulnerable. His hands could easily crush her, yet he relied on the dominating influence of his demanding kisses to obtain her surrender. He didn't take, but convinced her to give. He was a man hard enough to have a big heart.

"Edie, we've outgrown the stage of playing waiting games," he murmured, and lifted his head to frame her face with his large hands. His callused skin was pleasantly abrasive, a rough caress. "Leave that to Felicia and Jerry. We don't have any reason to play hard to get and those other games. It wastes too much precious time that we could be enjoying in other ways."

"I'm not playing any games." Her emotions were much too serious to be toyed with. She hoped he knew that.

"I want to make love to you, Edie." The determination in his voice started a fluttering in the pit of her stomach. "It's what you want, too. Don't try to deny it."

"I won't, Maddock." But she lowered her gaze to the leather stitching on his buckskin vest, feeling the tremors start.

"We've both been married. It isn't as if we don't know the score," he insisted, and lowered his hands to the sides of her neck, his thumbs caressing her throat. A stillness came over him as he felt the faint tremors quaking through her body. "You're trembling. What's wrong?"

"Nothing is wrong." Not really. It was more a case of nerves than anything else. It certainly wasn't a lack of wanting on her part. "It's just that I've never been to bed with any man other than my husband."

"I know that." He smiled into her uplifted gaze, but the puzzled light remained in his gray eyes.

"Don't you see?" The corners of her mouth deepened in a self-mocking smile. "It would be like the first time all over again."

A wondrous light flared in his eyes. "My God, Edie," he breathed and gathered her into his arms, rubbing his cheek against the softness of her hair. A shudder vibrated through his muscled frame. "That's the most beautiful thing you could have said to me."

"It isn't that I don't want you to make love to me, Maddock. It's just that I—" A pickup rumbled into the ranch yard. Edie drew back. "It must be Jerry coming home."

After taking a deep breath and releasing it, Maddock gave a wry shake of his head and let her go. Outside, a pair of truck doors slammed shut. "And I thought it was only married couples who were interrupted by inquisitive children," he murmured suggestively.

A smile was tugging at the corners of Edie's mouth when Alison burst into the house. "Mom, there's a strange car parked...outside." The last word was tacked belatedly on after Alison noticed Maddock standing near Edie. "What are you doing here?" Surprise increased her natural bluntness.

"I was just making sure your mother arrived home safely," Maddock replied, and exchanged a speaking glance with Edie.

"When I heard the truck," Edie spoke up to divert the subject, "I thought it was Jerry. I didn't expect to see you come through the door."

"Oh, Jerry's home, too." Alison glanced over her shoulder just as her half-brother entered the house. His glance stopped curiously on Maddock, too.

"You both came home together?" Edie looked at the two of them with faint surprise. "But I thought—"

"It made more sense for me to ride with Rob as far as the Diamond D Ranch and come home from there with Jerry after he'd dropped Felicia off," Alison explained the arrangement, then cocked her head to one side to study Maddock. "What happened to your face? It looks as if you've been in a fight?"

He touched the iodine-coated gash on his cheekbone as if he had forgotten the wound. "I fell down and cut myself," he lied blandly.

"It must have been some fall," Jerry observed skeptically. "You cut one cheek and bruised the jaw on the other side."

Edie knew they weren't going to be fooled by Maddock's story. "There was a very minor incident tonight," she admitted.

"What happened, mom?" Alison moved quickly to her side and Jerry followed.

Maddock answered the question. "Some young men were getting fresh with your mother. I merely reminded them of their manners." His glance ran over the three of them, standing together, side by side. Wry amusement flickered across his features. "The Three Musketeers are united again," he murmured.

"One for all and all for one," Alison returned brightly.

"I'm having a few friends over for a barbecue tomorrow. I'd like you to come." He looked at Edie as he offered the invitation, but his gaze quickly encompassed the three of them. "All of you."

Edie was aware of the shocked silence emanating from her daughter and stepson, but she felt absolutely no hesitation about accepting his invitation. So much had changed in the space of one evening. She simply couldn't regard Maddock as an enemy any longer.

"Thank you, Maddock. It sounds fun," she smiled under the intimate look in those gray eyes.

"Come early—around eleven-thirty. I want to show you around my home." The softness of his voice carried its own message.

Typically, he left without a goodbye, but Edie discovered she was becoming used to that. With his departure Jerry and Alison finally had a chance to voice their curiosity. Jerry was first.

"What's going on, Edie?" he frowned.

"Yes," Alison echoed his question. "Why do we suddenly rate an invitation to Sunday dinner?"

Edie had a lot of guesses of her own, but she only voiced the safest one. "Maybe he's finally decided that we are here to stay."

CHAPTER TEN

THE DIAMOND D ranch house was a white, two-story building with a pillared front. It faced the ranch buildings and had a spectacular view of the rough and broken Dakota terrain. This was Edie's first glimpse of the ranch headquarters, and she stared openly at its structures and network of corrals.

By the time Jerry had parked the car in front of the house, Maddock was outside to greet them. "Welcome to the Diamond D." He reserved a warm look for Edie. "I'm sorry Felicia isn't on hand to greet you, but she's still upstairs getting ready. Come inside."

His hand rested in light possession on the back of her waist as he personally escorted Edie to the front door with Jerry and Alison trailing behind them. The foyered entrance to the house included a staircase to the second floor. To the right, decorated in soft rusts and golds, was the living room where Maddock began his tour of the house. A fireplace built of native stone gave the room a relaxed, comfortable air.

"There are three fireplaces in the house, two

downstairs and one upstairs," Maddock explained as he led them into the dining room.

There was an informal quality about the room. It was easy for Edie to imagine Maddock sitting at the head of a tableful of guests, discussing the ranch or politics or something as basic as Johnny's first tooth. Despite the richness of the solid walnut table, chairs and sideboard, there was something essentially casual about the room.

A cook was busy in the kitchen with preparations for the noon barbecue, so they didn't linger long there. But Edie did notice it was equipped with all the latest conveniences, with plenty of work space and a breakfast nook.

The last room he showed them on the ground floor was the den, paneled in knotty pine with leather-upholstered furniture. The bookshelves were lined with volumes on animal husbandry and agriculture interspersed with a selection of novels. Issues of ranch-related magazines were scattered around the room, giving it a lived-in look. A second fireplace was located in the den, constructed of burned brick.

As they returned to the foyer, Edie realized this was definitely a rancher's house where a man could feel free to walk in straight from the ranch yard without worrying greatly about what he tracked onto the floors. He could bring in a newborn calf, half-frozen by a winter's storm, and let the warmth of the kitchen nurse it back to life. Despite its imposing size, it was a home.

"We'll have the barbecue on the patio in the backyard by the pool." He paused beside the thermo-paned glass doors that opened from the foyer onto the patio. "Last night I forgot to suggest that you bring your swimming suits along, but there's a small selection of styles and sizes that we keep on hand for guests in the changing room."

"Look!" Alison pointed to an object out of Edie's sight. "There's Rob."

"Yes," Maddock affirmed her statement. "He's helping set up the tables."

"Let's give him a hand, Jerry." Alison was quick to find a reason to see him again.

"Go ahead," Maddock nodded when Jerry hesitated to agree with his half-sister's suggestion. "We'll be out shortly." As the two slid open the glass doors, the hand on Edie's back applied pressure to steer her away from the doors. Maddock wandered, apparently aimlessly, to the center of the foyer. "That concludes the tour of the house, with the exception of the upstairs," he corrected with a glance at the staircase. "There are five bedrooms in all, counting the master suite." He turned her around to face him, resting his hands on her hips. "What do you think of it?"

"Between the house and the ranch buildings, I'm convinced we'll never be able to approach your scale of operation," Edie admitted. "If your intention was to impress me, you've succeeded."

His mouth thinned with displeasure. Her reply wasn't the one he wanted to hear. "I'm not interested in impressing you. I want to know what you think of my home. Is it someplace you'd like to live? Do you like it?"

"I like it, yes." Edie hesitated to say more, certain she was reading more into his question than Maddock intended.

"That's why I wanted you to come today—so you could see where I live and get to know my friends. It probably seems like I'm rushing things...and I am," he admitted with a flash of wry amusement. "But I know what I want, Edie. I want to marry you. I want you to be my wife."

"Maddock." Amazement, a wondrous kind of disbelief and a little shock became all mixed up in the issuance of his name. She hadn't expected a proposal! She knew the answer she wanted to give him, but the words wouldn't come out.

He gazed into her eyes, shining with happiness, and read her answer. A slow smile of satisfaction curved his firmly cut mouth. His head started to bend toward her and stopped when he heard car doors slam outside and voices signaling the approach of guests.

Before the arriving guests reached the front door, he claimed her lips in a hard, possessive kiss that revealed his desire and frustration. She clung to his kiss for an instant, then let him draw away.

"We'll talk about this later—after everyone has left," he told her as someone knocked on the door. But the light in his gray eyes promised there would be less talking and more action.

When he left her to welcome his guests at the door, Edie was lost in a bliss-filled daze. A faint noise came from the stairs and Edie turned. Felicia Maddock stood poised on the steps halfway down. It became quickly evident to Edie that the girl had been there for some time. She saw the cold hurt of jealousy in the girl's blue eyes as they bored into her. Ignoring her father at the door with the arriving friends, Felicia came swinging down the steps directly toward Edie. Her expression was coldly haughty.

"I knew daddy wanted your ranch," Felicia murmured. "But it never occurred to me he wanted it badly enough to marry *you* to get it."

With her poisoned barb delivered, Felicia swept past, not allowing Edie a chance to reply. In numbed shock she watched the girl walk to Maddock's side to gaily welcome their guests. Was it possible that the motive behind Maddock's proposal was to obtain control of the ranch?

When Maddock called her forward to introduce her to his friends, Edie knew it wasn't true. Maddock fought for what he wanted and fought hard, but he wasn't the kind to resort to underhanded tactics. He was too blunt, too forthright.

No, Felicia had deliberately implanted that

seed of doubt, hoping it would germinate and grow when nourished by Edie's fertile imagination. The ranch had always been a wedge between Edie and Maddock, and Felicia wanted to keep it that way. But she'd made a mistake, because Edie knew Maddock too well to believe that about him.

Maddock kept Edie at his side as he led his party of guests outside to the patio. She managed to take an absent part in the conversation swirling around her and answer questions put to her by his friends, but her thoughts kept running back to Felicia.

Halfway through the meal of barbecued ribs and chicken, it occurred to Edie why Felicia had made such a vicious remark. It had been jealousy she'd seen in the girl's expression. For years she had been the only female in her father's life, spoiled and pampered and indulged by him. Felicia was the mistress of the house.

If Maddock married Edie, all that would change. Felicia felt threatened. Edie would not only upset her position as lady of the house, but she would also become the object of her father's affection and attention. And, childlike, Felicia didn't want to share him. Felicia resented Edie, just as she would resent any woman that she felt might come between her and her father.

The situation troubled Edie. Knowing the problem did not automatically provide a solution. There had to be a way to handle it if she just had time to think, but that was impossible with so many people around.

After everyone had finished their meal, there was a general disinclination to move from the tables. When Edie noticed Felicia at the buffet table to replenish her iced tea, she saw an opportunity to speak to the girl.

"I'm going to get some more iced tea," she murmured her excuse to Maddock, and rose from the table. She crossed the patio to the end of the buffet where the insulated urn of iced tea was located. When Felicia saw her approach, she started to walk away. "Felicia," Edie called out quickly to stop the girl. "I'd like to speak to you for a moment."

"I can't think of a thing that we would possibly have to say to one another," the girl replied with obvious disdain.

"There is something we need to get straightened out," Edie insisted quietly but firmly. "I think you have misunderstood some things."

"No, you are the one who doesn't understand," Felicia retorted. Edie saw Jerry and Alison approaching the buffet table, but Felicia's back was to them and she was unaware there was anyone within hearing except Edie. "Daddy and I have tried to make it clear to you from the beginning. You aren't wanted here. You never have been. Regardless of what you might think now, that hasn't changed."

"Felicia," Edie tried to warn the girl that Alison and Jerry were listening. Anger had already turned Jerry's mouth grim and brought the fighting sparks to Alison's eyes.

"You wanted to talk," the girl reminded her that the conversation had been Edie's idea. "So you might as well listen to some advice. You've had your free meal, so why don't you leave?"

"I think that's an excellent idea, mother," Alison spoke up, and Felicia pivoted in surprise. "I know when I'm not wanted."

"Jerry!" Felicia gasped in dismay.

"I always knew you were a spoiled, selfish brat," he said tightly. "You've grown way too big for your britches."

Before anyone could guess his intention, Jerry scooped Felicia off her feet and into his arms. She shrieked in alarm, but didn't struggle too hard to get free. Edie sunk her teeth into her lower lip as she realized that everyone at the barbecue was watching them, including Maddock, who had stood up.

"Jerry, put me down!" Felicia protested, but he continued to walk, carrying her in his arms. "What *are* you doing?"

Edie had already guessed when she noticed that he was walking toward the swimming pool. An instant later Felicia reached the same conclusion. She screamed something about him ruining her dress, but it was too late. He was at the edge of the pool and heaving her into the water. Jerry waited long enough to see her sputter to the surface, then turned to rejoin Edie and Alison.

"I think we'd better leave," he said to Edie above the confused laughter and the rush of people to the pool to help Felicia out of the water. Maddock was among them.

Under the circumstances, Edie felt leaving was the wisest choice. "Yes, I think we should." Explanations would have to be made to Maddock, but it could be done later. This was not the time.

"I wish I had a picture of that," Alison murmured as they entered the house through the sliding doors. "Only you could do that and get away with it, Jerry."

"She needed to be turned upside down and spanked," he muttered.

"I feel sorry for her. She's so confused and insecure." Edie sighed and glanced at the staircase rising from the foyer.

"Felicia?" Alison gave her a wide look. "Are you sure we're talking about the same girl?"

"Yes, I—". Edie wasn't able to finish her explanation as the sliding glass doors to the patio opened behind them. All three glanced back when they heard it.

Maddock came striding across the entry hall. "Where the hell do you think you're going?" The low demand was taut and angry, the hard steel of his gaze directed at Edie.

Alison and Jerry immediately closed ranks around her, providing a united front. "Under the circumstances, Maddock, we thought it was best to leave," Edie explained.

"I suggest that you change your mind," he ordered tersely. "You are staying here."

"We don't take orders," Alison retorted. "Certainly not from you."

"Edie had nothing to do with what happened by the pool," Jerry stated, moving forward to take the brunt of Maddock's anger. "I was the one who threw Felicia in the water. And I'm not going to apologize for it, either. She deserved worse than that for the things she said to Edie."

Maddock's stone-gray eyes flicked over Jerry and Alison with hard impatience. "This is a private discussion between Edie and myself. You have no business interfering in it."

"Maddock—" Edie bristled at his censuring tone as the air crackled with tension.

"Be quiet, Edie," he snapped. "I'm going to get this straightened out once and for all. There will be plenty of times in the future when I'll be raising my voice at you over something. There isn't any way that every time we argue, I'm going to take on the whole Gibbs family. It's time they learned to keep out of any discussion between a man and his wife!"

"His wife?" Alison frowned and glanced at Edie. "What's he talking about, mom?"

"This isn't the way I wanted you to find out," Edie said, and flashed an irritated glance at Maddock. Everything had mushroomed out of control. "He asked me to marry him." Just saying the words seemed to make it more real

In spite of her defensive anger, her voice softened as she made the announcement.

"Are you?" was Alison's instant and slightly incredulous reaction.

But Jerry had been watching her expression and noticed the way her gaze had sought Maddock when she told them. He guessed what her answer had been and bent his head to kiss her cheek. "Dad would be happy for you, Edie," he said to ease her mind. "I'm glad you found somebody else, too." He smiled, then turned to Maddock and offered his hand. "Congratulations. You've got yourself quite a woman."

"Yes, I know." His roughly hewn features were gentled by the warmth of his look as Maddock held Edie's gaze. The possessive light burning in his gray eyes started a tingling in her nerve ends.

For Alison, none of it had truly sunk in. She glanced around in helpless confusion. "I don't understand," she murmured.

"I'll explain it to her," Jerry smiled at Edie and took his sister by the hand to lead her away so Edie could be alone with Maddock. "It's this way, Alison," he began as they walked away. "There is this emotion called love."

Edie didn't hear any more than that as his voice trailed away. Maddock had taken a step toward her, his large hands settling onto her shoulders while his gaze searched her face.

"Don't ever walk away like that again, Edie." This time it was a request. "Why did you do it? You know I asked you to stay until the others had left."

"Yes," she admitted, her voice growing soft. "But after that incident with Felicia—"

"What on earth did she say to you?" An amused frown flickered across his forehead. "It was all I could do to keep from laughing when Jerry dumped her in the pool."

"It doesn't really matter what she said," Edie insisted.

"Yes, it does, if it was something against you," Maddock corrected firmly.

She realized it would all come out sooner or later. "She doesn't want you to marry me."

"I know." There was a wry twist to his mouth. "When I told her this morning, she threw a tantrum. That's why she was upstairs sulking when you arrived."

"Felicia tried to convince me that the only reason you wanted to marry me was to get the ranch," Edie admitted.

His hands tightened on her shoulders as his gaze became piercing. "You didn't believe that? Is that why you were leaving?"

"No." She smiled and shook her head. "You may want our ranch, but I don't think you would go to the extreme of marrying me just to get your hands on it. It wouldn't work, anyway."

"I never for a minute thought it would." His look gentled. "I'm sure that you plan to turn the ranch over to Jerry and Alison after we're married. But I still don't think any of you realize the mammoth job you're tackling before the ranch will show a profit."

"There's something you don't know about us." Her eyes danced with the one fact they had kept from him. "Joe left us an income independent of the ranch. We weren't gambling all of our money."

"I should have known," Maddock chuckled. "I think I stopped caring about getting the ranch when you outsmarted me and bought those cattle in Wyoming. That's just about the time I started falling in love with you, too."

She caught her breath, a sudden radiance shining in her expression. "Do you realize that is the first time you've told me that, Will Maddock?"

"Told you what? That I love you?" His gaze roamed over her face. "I thought I'd been telling you that every time I looked at you."

"You have," she said softly. "But it's nice to hear the actual words."

An encircling arm pulled her against his rugged frame while his large hand became tangled in her hair. She melted against him, her lips parting as his mouth moved over them in clear possession. Joy sang through her veins, pure and sweet, a pleasure so strong that she hadn't believed it could exist. The depth of her love for him left Edie breathless. Her hands were spread across his broad back, feeling the tautly rigid muscles.

Maddock finally called a halt to the kiss before it went out of control. His breathing was as heavy as her own as he lifted his head. Raw desire smoldered in the look that scanned her love-soft features.

"We're going to be married next week, Edie," he informed her. "If I could arrange it, it would be this afternoon."

"But what about Felicia?" She gently reminded him of his daughter's disapproval. "Maybe we should give her time to get used to the idea."

"Time isn't going to help her...and it would be hell for me," he declared with a wicked glint in his eyes. "I haven't done a very good job of raising my daughter. She needs you as much as I do—well, almost as much as I do," he qualified his statement.

"It isn't going to be easy for her," Edie warned, and caressed his hard cheek. "She's used to being the only woman in your life."

"I think Jerry can handle that problem." The corners of his mouth deepened with a smile. "I have the feeling that ranch is going to wind up in the Maddock family yet."

"You are incorrigible!" she laughed.

"No, I'm in love. And that can be contagious," he replied.

"It certainly can," she agreed and lifted her lips to receive his.

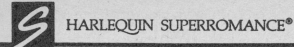

WELCOME TO

The quintessential small town,
where everyone knows everybody else!

Each book set in Tyler is a self-contained love story; together,
the twelve novels stitch the fabric of the community.

"Scintillating romance!"
"Immensely appealing characters... wonderful intensity and
humor."
Romantic Times

Join your friends in Tyler for the ninth book,
MILKY WAY by Muriel Jensen, available in November.

*Can Jake help solve Britt's family financial problems and win her love?
Was Margaret's death really murder?*

GREAT READING...GREAT SAVINGS...AND A
FABULOUS FREE GIFT!

With Tyler you can receive a fabulous gift, ABSOLUTELY FREE,
by collecting proofs-of-purchase found in each Tyler book.
And use our special Tyler coupons to save on your next
TYLER book purchase.

· HARLEQUIN ·
HISTORICAL

CHRISTMAS

· STORIES · 1992 ·

Capture the magic and romance of Christmas in the 1800s
with HARLEQUIN HISTORICAL CHRISTMAS STORIES
1992—a collection of three stories by celebrated
historical authors. The perfect Christmas gift!

Don't miss these heartwarming stories, available in
November wherever Harlequin books are sold:

**MISS MONTRACHET REQUESTS by Maura Seger
CHRISTMAS BOUNTY by Erin Yorke
A PROMISE KEPT by Bronwyn Williams**

Plus, this Christmas you can also receive a FREE
keepsake Christmas ornament. Watch for details in all
November and December Harlequin books.

**DISCOVER THE ROMANCE AND MAGIC OF THE
HOLIDAY SEASON WITH HARLEQUIN HISTORICAL
CHRISTMAS STORIES!**

HX92R

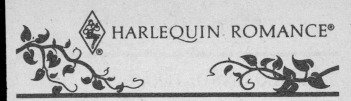

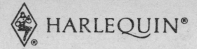